T
Amorous Ambassador

An American Farce

by

Michael Parker

SAMUEL FRENCH, INC.

45 WEST 25TH STREET — NEW YORK 10010
7623 SUNSET BOULEVARD — HOLLYWOOD 90046
LONDON — *TORONTO*

ISBN 0 573 67040 4 Printed in U.S.A. #3157

IMPORTANT BILLING AND CREDIT REQUIREMENTS

All producers of THE AMOROUS AMBASSADOR *must* give credit to the Author of the Play in all programs distributed in connection with performances of the Play and in all instances in which the title of the Play appears for purposes of advertising, publicizing or otherwise exploiting the Play and/or a production. The name of the Author *must* also appear on a separate line, on which no other name appears, immediately following the title, and *must* appear in size of type not less than fifty percent the size of the title type.

THE AMOROUS AMBASSADOR

First produced at the Delray Beach Playhouse, Delray Beach, Florida on November 29, 1990, with the following cast:

PERKINS . . . . Michael Parker
DEBBIE DOUGLAS . . . . Nedria DeGrotta
HARRY DOUGLAS . . . . Jack Gordon
LOIS DOUGLAS . . . . Joan Blumenreich
MARIAN MURDOCH . . . . Diane DuMar
JOE . . . . Chuck Tisdale
CAPTAIN SOUTH . . . . Kevin John Duncan
FAYE BAKER . . . . Andrea Rosenfield

Directed by: Randolph DelLago
Designed by: Ann Cadaret

CHARACTERS

HARRY DOUGLAS:

A former U.S. Senator, now the U.S. Ambassador to Britain. A philanderer and woman chaser, he usually manages to smooth-talk his way out of compromising situations. Suave, elegant, good looking. Age 45-65.

PERKINS:

The quintessential butler. A pivotal character around whom most of the circumstantial humor seems to occur. He remains "Oh so British", never cracks a smile and always seems to be in control. Age 50+.

JOE:

Joe's great misfortune in life is that his girlfriend (Debbie) is the Ambassador's daughter. He is caught up in a whirlwind of events, and never seems to understand how he has got into such a mess. He spends a good portion of the play in a dress and wig, pretending to be Debbie's girlfriend, Josephine, fighting off the advances of "The Amorous Ambassador". Age 20-30.

CAPTAIN SOUTH:

The Marine Corps officer in charge of embassy security. He is a total incompetent, who spends his time searching for a non-existent "mad bomber", when he is not being knocked out, hit by doors, etc. Age 25-45.

DEBBIE:

The Ambassador's daughter, a bright, attractive young lady, whose quick thinking keeps her one step ahead of her father, as she manipulates all those around her. Age 20-25.

MARIAN:

The Ambassador's girl-friend from next door, is beautiful, glamorous and sexy. Her costumes range from a cocktail dress, and a French maid's outfit to lingerie. Age 25-40.

FAYE:

The Ambassador's secretary, is not too bright. In fact, when Harry suggests she hold a seance to see if she can make contact with her brain, it's probably a good idea. She breaks things, she drops things, she is a living, breathing, walking disaster area. Age 25-40.

LOIS DOUGLAS:

Harry's long suffering wife who manages to turn the tables on him, in the final unexpected denouement. Age 40+.

The action of the play takes place in the country home of the United States Ambassador to Britain, outside London.

ACT I:
An early Friday evening in summer.

ACT II:
(Scene One) The action is continuous.
(Scene Two) Later the same evening.

ACT I

(The curtain rises on an empty set. It is the living room of an English country house, The room is tastefully furnished in typical English style with drapes, rugs, books, china, etc.)

(Down R. is bedroom #2 and above it the door to bedroom #1. Between these two doors is a small table or dresser with a mirror above it. Up R.C. are French windows opening on to a small patio, with a low stone wall and garden beyond. The exit from the patio to the garden is R. Up C. is a sideboard or credenza with glasses, drinks, etc. Up L. is the front door with a garden setting outside. R. of the front door is a coat stand with a man's raincoat, Lois' suit jacket and purse on it. L.C. is the door to the kitchen, which is double hinged, and down L. the door to the study. Against the wall L. between the kitchen and study doors is a desk facing the audience with a telephone and a small vase of fresh flowers. R.C. is a sofa [which must pull out into a sofa-bed] with a coffee table in front. L.C. is a low backed easy chair.)

(After a moment's silence PERKINS enters from the kitchen with a jug of lemonade which he places on the credenza.)

(PERKINS is the epitome of the English butler. Perhaps 50, graying, ramrod straight, always serious, never smiling, always formal, never relaxed. He wears gray pinstripe trousers, dark vest, white shirt with long sleeves and a black tie. He moves behind the desk and "reverses" the

telephone receiver, then moves the phone carefully about half an inch. He then notices one of the sofa cushions is not quite straight. He crosses to the sofa and straightens it. He then backs off L. and bends down to see if they are straight. Now another cushion is not exactly "lined up". He moves it and backs off L. closing one eye to see if the cushions are now absolutely perfect, as DEBBIE enters from BR2. She is in her early twenties, pretty, bright, intelligent and wearing a floral print summer dress.)

DEBBIE: Oh, hi Perkins.

PERKINS: *(Very formal and with an almost imperceptible bow)* Good evening Miss Deborah.

DEBBIE: *(Heading L. behind the sofa towards the credenza)* I'm ready for a drink.

PERKINS: *(Placing himself between her and the credenza)* May I get it for you Miss Deborah?

DEBBIE: *(Stops)* Oh. Yes. O.K. I'll have a small martini, thank you.

PERKINS: If you would please be seated miss, I shall attend to it immediately.

(Turns to the credenza and starts to mix drinks.)

DEBBIE: *(Sits R. end of the sofa with one leg tucked underneath her)* You know, I'm not sure I'll ever get used to having a butler around.

PERKINS: Well, I've only been here two weeks. I'm sure that in time you'll be able to make the adjustment.

DEBBIE: It's just that in America, even when my father was a senator in Washington, long before he became ambassador to Britain, we never had people living in our house – other than family I mean.

PERKINS: I'm sure we shall get on famously miss.

DEBBIE: What's it like being a butler?

PERKINS: I beg your pardon.

DEBBIE: I mean, don't you get tired of living in someone else's house?

PERKINS: *(Coming D.R. with her drink on a small silver tray)* Not at all miss. As you no doubt know, I live in my quarters above the garage at the end of the garden. The apartment, *(He stops in mid sentence and looks disapprovingly at DEBBIE's posture. She looks at him, realizes why he is looking at her, and quickly sits properly on the couch)* though quite small, is very comfortable. I work here in this house, though I must say this is a much smaller household than I've been used to.

DEBBIE: Oh really. Where did you work before?

PERKINS: Actually I was the butler to Lord Birkby for nearly thirty years.

DEBBIE: Good heavens! Why did you leave him?

PERKINS: In a manner of speaking miss, he left me.

DEBBIE: What do you mean?

PERKINS: He died.

DEBBIE: Oh I see. I'm sorry. *(She gets up and looks around)* Perkins?

PERKINS: Yes miss?

DEBBIE: Do you know where my father is?

PERKINS: The ambassador and your mother are taking a stroll around the garden. Excuse me please.

(He turns and heads towards the kitchen.)

DEBBIE: Perkins! Please don't go. *(He stops)* There's something I'd like to discuss with you.

PERKINS: *(Turning)* Yes miss?

DEBBIE: *(Goes to the French windows, looks out, makes sure the coast is clear and turns)* Well, I'm not sure how best to put this. *(Pause. Perkins looks blank, offering no help at all)* The thing is – I wondered if – er – you know – if there were to be someone here, how discreet about it would you be?

PERKINS: *(Perplexed)* Someone here? Discreet? I'm afraid you're going to have to be more specific miss.

DEBBIE: Right. *(Pacing a little)* Take your previous employer for example.

PERKINS: Lord Birkby?

DEBBIE: Yes. Now, did he have any children?

PERKINS: Yes miss.

DEBBIE: A daughter?

PERKINS: Yes miss.

DEBBIE: Good. Now supposing his daughter had a boyfriend who visited her, and – er – you know – stayed – well – er – overnight. *(Perkins reacts)* Would you have told Lord Birkby?

PERKINS: The situation could not possibly have occurred.

DEBBIE: Oh – and why not?

PERKINS: In the first place, prior to his Lordship's death, his daughter hadn't lived at home in twenty years, and in the second place –

DEBBIE: Yes?

PERKINS: She's a Carmelite nun!

DEBBIE: Oh dear – I see, but you do understand what I'm getting at?

PERKINS: Perfectly miss, and I'm glad of the opportunity to explain to you my position in this household. Your father, the ambassador, is my employer, and I will not under any circumstances lie to him. But, neither am I here to volunteer information to him about his family. You may therefore count on me to be the absolute soul of discretion.

DEBBIE: That's wonderful! Thank you Perkins – and – er – not a word to "you know who"?

PERKINS: Not a word miss. Now, if you'll excuse me, I have work to do in the kitchen.

(Exit to kitchen. DEBBIE does a little dance of joy, and blows kisses to the kitchen door.)

(Enter HARRY through the French windows. He is a distinguished looking man, age 50 to 60 with gray hair. He wears slacks, a long sleeved shirt and tie, but no jacket.)

HARRY: Hi Debbie.

DEBBIE: Oh hi Dad.

HARRY: *(Goes to the credenza)* Want something?

DEBBIE: No thanks, Perkins already got me one.

(Sits on the couch.)

HARRY: *(Pouring himself a drink and chuckling)* He's really something that Perkins eh?

DEBBIE: Dad?

HARRY: Yeah?

DEBBIE: Why did you hire a butler?

HARRY: Ah, in actual fact I didn't. The State

Department did. The point is, sooner of later, we're going to have to do some entertaining here, as well as at the embassy, and you know what the Brits are like for proper protocol and etiquette. I guess they feel an English butler will make sure we do all the right things at the right times. *(He takes his drink and sits in the chair)* In any case, you must admit he adds a touch of class to the place.

DEBBIE: I suppose so. Wasn't Mom with you in the garden?

HARRY: Yes. She's pruning the roses. She's becoming more English than the English. Can you imagine – pruning the roses?

DEBBIE: *(Laughs)* Dear old Mom, she really likes it here doesn't she?

HARRY: She's having the time of her life. She's off this weekend to – er – what did she call it – a health and fitness spa.

DEBBIE: You mean a fat farm don't you?

HARRY: Yes, but don't let her hear you call it that.

DEBBIE: What are you going to do?

HARRY: Well, when you said you were going to your girlfriend's for the weekend, I didn't like the idea of being here all alone, so I fixed up a golf weekend. Four of us are going to Scotland, won't be back till Sunday night.

DEBBIE: Actually, Mom mentioned it to me. So – we're all going to be away for the whole weekend.

HARRY: Looks like it.

DEBBIE: *(Getting up)* Well, I think I'll just throw a few things into a suitcase and be on my way.

(Exits BR2.)

HARRY: *(Gets up and looks out of the French windows, makes sure the coast is clear, crosses to the kitchen door and opens it slightly)* Perkins, could I see you for a moment please?

(Crosses R. behind the sofa.)

PERKINS: *(Enters and stands by the kitchen door)* Yes sir?

HARRY: Perkins. There's something I'd like to discuss with you.

PERKINS: Yes sir.

HARRY: Well now, as you know, I'm going to play golf in Scotland this weekend.

PERKINS: Yes sir.

HARRY: Well, there might be a change of plans.

PERKINS: Really, sir?

HARRY: *(Pacing)* Yes, but we don't need to mention it to anyone do we?

PERKINS: Not if you say so sir.

HARRY: I do – I do. Now – er – if this change of plans were to take place – *(Pause)* – I'm not sure how best to put this – *(PERKINS looks blank, offering no help at all)* The thing is – I wondered if – you know – if there were to be someone here – how discreet about it would you be?

PERKINS: *(With just a hint of a smile)* Someone here? Discreet? I'm afraid you're going to have to be more specific sir.

HARRY: Right. *(Pause)* You ever been married Perkins?

PERKINS: No sir.

HARRY: Ah-well. You'll find it hard to understand then.

PERKINS: Understand what sir?

HARRY: Understand that wives don't understand.

PERKINS: Understand that wives don't understand what sir?

HARRY: Dammit Perkins! How shall I put this? Let's take your previous employers for example.

PERKINS: Lord and Lady Birkby sir?

HARRY: Exactly. Now – er – er.

PERKINS: Would it help if I told you their daughter lived in a convent?

HARRY: What?

PERKINS: I think perhaps we can abbreviate this conversation if we were to skip right to the part where I say "You may count on me to be the absolute soul of discretion".

HARRY: I can?

PERKINS: Yes indeed sir.

HARRY: Excellent, and – er – not a word to "you know who"?

PERKINS: Not a word sir. Will that be all?

HARRY: Yes, thank you Perkins. *(Exit PERKINS to kitchen)* Absolutely amazing, *(Mimicking PERKINS' English accent)* "You may count on me to be the absolute soul of discretion". *(He goes to the French windows)* Lois. Lois. *(Enter LOIS. 50-ish neat tidy, quite a handsome woman dressed in a conservative two piece suit minus jacket, and flat shoes)* What time is your train my love?

LOIS: *(Looking at her watch and coming into the living room)* Oh I've got plenty of time, I don't need to be at the station till six-thirty.

HARRY: Can I drop you off?

LOIS: *(Taking off a pair of gardening gloves which she*

puts on the small table R. along with a pair of shears) Thank you Harry, that's very sweet of you, but Debbie said she'd take me on the way to town. I've got about ten minutes and I'm all packed. I think I'll have some of that delicious lemonade Perkins makes.

(She goes toward the credenza.)

HARRY: Allow me my love!

(He goes to the credenza.)

LOIS: Thank you my sweet. *(Comes D. and sits on the couch)* You know Harry, I'm so glad the State Department bought this place. I like living in London, of course, but it's so nice to get into the country on the weekends.

HARRY: *(Brings her lemonade)* I know what you mean. It's rather funny though isn't it. All three of us going to be away from here this weekend.

(Sits in chair.)

LOIS: Talking of being away for the weekend, what time will you be leaving?

HARRY: Oh, I thought I'd head out as soon as I've seen you and Debbie safely off.

LOIS: And you won't be back till Sunday evening?

HARRY: That's right my love. By the way, when will you get back?

LOIS: I'm not sure what time on Sunday they let us escape. Probably late afternoon. I wonder if Debbie is going to see that new boyfriend of hers. You know Harry, she's reaching the age when she ought to be thinking about getting married and settling down.

HARRY: *(Smiles)* That's your answer to all life's problems isn't it? I swear, if you met the Pope, you'd probably tell him to get married and settle down.

LOIS: Well, Debbie's the same age I was when we got married, and her last boyfriend was so nice. I really thought he might be the one.

HARRY: Oh, he was O.K. I suppose. I thought he was a bit young and naive though.

LOIS: He was just a bit shy. I think he'd led a sheltered life and anyway that's why I liked him.

HARRY: Sheltered life? That's the understatement of the year. I do believe his only experience with the opposite sex had been the centerfold of magazines. I bet it will come as a great surprise to him when he discovers women don't have a staple across their middle.

LOIS: *(Laughing)* Oh Harry! You know I think I'd better have Perkins prepare a cold buffet for Sunday evening.

HARRY: Take it easy on Perkins my dear. Remember he only took the job on the understanding we would hire a maid. So, until we find one, don't overload him.

LOIS: He's hardly overloaded dear. We haven't done any entertaining here at all. Come to think of it, we really ought to invite some of the neighbors around. We've been here two weeks, it's time we met them.

HARRY: Perhaps next weekend dear.

LOIS: Have you met any of them?

HARRY: *(Suddenly flustered)* Er – who – what?

LOIS: The neighbors dear.

HARRY: Ah yes. The lady next door.

LOIS: What's she like?

HARRY: *(Gazing rapturously into space)* Ravishing!

LOIS: I beg your pardon.

HARRY: Fishing – hunting – shooting type you know.

LOIS: I see. What's her name?

HARRY: Marian, Marian Murdoch.

LOIS: Oh well. As you say, we must do it next weekend. By the way, I've laid out your shirts and underwear on the bed dear.

HARRY: *(Getting up)* Right, I'll go and pack then.

(Exits BR1.)

LOIS: *(Waits till HARRY is safely in the bedroom then crosses to the kitchen, opens the door and calls)* Perkins.

(She steps back behind the chair.)

PERKINS: *(Entering)* Yes madam?

LOIS: *(Pacing nervously)* There's something I'd like to discuss with you.

PERKINS: Yes madam?

LOIS: Well – er – this is a little difficult. I'm not sure how best to put this.

PERKINS: Perhaps it would help if I were to tell you his daughter is a nun, I have never been married, wives don't understand, you can count on me to be the absolute soul of discretion and not a word to you know who.

LOIS: I see. *(Pause)* Are you what they call an eccentric Englishman?

PERKINS: Not at all madam. I just like to get to the crux of the matter.

DEBBIE: *(Enters from BR2 with a small suitcase and crosses to the L. of the front door)* You about ready Mom?

LOIS: Yes dear, I'll just get my bag.

PERKINS: *(Moves to the door of BR1)* Allow me madam.

(HE goes into BR1.)

LOIS: *(Putting on her suit jacket, and taking her purse from the coat stand)* Don't you think you ought to take a sweater? It gets quite cool in the evenings you know.

DEBBIE: I'll be just fine Mom.

LOIS: Well I don't want you to catch cold or something.

DEBBIE: Mom, stop fussing.

LOIS: Alright dear.

(Enter PERKINS from BR1 carrying a small suitcase, followed by HARRY.)

HARRY: Have a nice weekend dear.

LOIS: You too Harry. *(She gives him a peck on the cheek)* I hope you get good weather for your golf.

DEBBIE: You all packed Dad?

HARRY: Yes, I'll be out of here myself in a few minutes. I'll just see you to the car.

(He takes LOIS' suitcase from PERKINS. LOIS, DEBBIE and HARRY exit front door.)

(PERKINS who has opened the front door, stands motionless looking after them.)

LOIS: *(Off)* I shall miss you my love.

HARRY: *(Off)* The weekend will seem like an eternity without you my sweet. *(PERKINS rolls his eyes heavenward, closes the front door and exits to kitchen. After a brief pause, the front door opens to reveal HARRY. He strikes a pose in the doorway, then, singing softly to himself, closes the front door, rubs his hands together, does a little jig, briefly listens at the kitchen door then picks up the phone and dials)* Hello sweetiekins! How's my very favorite, gorgeous, delectable, sensational, sexy next door neighbor? Can your hormones come out to play? Are you ready for that wild abandoned weekend we planned? It's all arranged, Lois is off to eat lettuce leaves or something and Debbie's gone to her girlfriend's. So we have the place to ourselves till Sunday night – Oh yes – Perkins – I'd almost forgotten him – don't worry about a thing – I'll get rid of him, give me five minutes and come through the garden. *(Enter PERKINS from the kitchen, he carries a tray and crosses to pick up the empty glasses from the coffee table)* Er – yes, please tell Mr. Major that Hillary says Bill will call him when he has the time. Thank you, good-bye. *(He hurriedly hangs up the phone)* Ah, Perkins, I've been thinking. I'll probably be leaving soon and as there won't be anyone here, why don't you take the whole weekend off?

PERKINS: Well I just thought I'd tidy up a little sir.

(Takes the glasses and puts them on the tray which he takes to the credenza.)

HARRY: The place looks tidy enough to me.

PERKINS: Yes sir, that's why you are an ambassador and not a butler.

(Now back to the sofa, fluffing and straightening cushions.)

HARRY: I know. Why don't you go into London for the weekend?

PERKINS: Whatever for sir?

HARRY: Well, you could see a show or visit an art gallery or something. I believe there's a Rubens exhibition on at the National Gallery.

PERKINS: The thought of looking at paintings of naked women with large bottoms and small breasts eating fruit *(He pauses in anticipation)* does not appeal to me, thank you sir.

HARRY: Dammit Perkins! I'm trying to say I want you out of the house this evening.

PERKINS: But I thought you were going to Scotland to play golf sir.

HARRY: That's the idea. Everybody thinks I'm playing golf in Scotland.

PERKINS: Ah – I think perhaps I understand sir. I take it then that you're not?

HARRY: Not what?

PERKINS: Not playing golf in Scotland.

HARRY: Exactly. Now you've got the picture.

PERKINS: *(Pause)* Is this where my absolute discretion comes in sir?

HARRY: Now you're cooking.

PERKINS: I never cook sir! Actually, I intend to have a cold supper this evening.

HARRY: And not a word to "you know who"?

PERKINS: Very well sir. I'll just make myself a sandwich to take to my apartment.

(Turns towards the kitchen.)

HARRY: There's just one more thing Perkins.

PERKINS: Yes sir?

HARRY: Do we have any caviar?

PERKINS: Yes indeed sir.

HARRY: Get a couple of jars out please and leave them in the kitchen.

PERKINS: Yes sir. Would there be anything else?

HARRY: Yes. Put some champagne in an ice bucket would you.

PERKINS: Not the Dom Perignon from the wine cupboard in the study?

HARRY: Perfect!

(Exit PERKINS to the study. HARRY gives a little skip, breaks into song again and exits to BR1.)

(Enter MARIAN through the French windows, carrying a small package. She is 35-40 beautiful and voluptuous. A little overdressed in a cocktail gown with a plunging neckline, but the picture is one of sensuality, sophistication and grace. She can be English or American.)

MARIAN: *(Calling as she enters)* Harry – Harry!

(She comes down to the rear of the sofa.)

PERKINS: *(Re-entering from the study with the bottle of champagne)* Good evening madam. May I help you?

MARIAN: Well, actually I was looking for Mr. Douglas.

PERKINS: *(Crossing R. U.S.)* Ah yes. May I tell him who's calling?

MARIAN: Miss Murdoch from next door. I just dropped in.

PERKINS: *(To no one in particular)* I must say the old bastard's got a beauty.

MARIAN: What's that?

PERKINS: I said the ambassador's not on duty.

(Enter HARRY from BR1.)

HARRY: Ah – welcome Marian. I see you've already met Perkins.

MARIAN: Yes. *(Whispers)* Harry, you told me you'd get rid of him.

HARRY: I know dear. *(Turns to PERKINS)* Perkins is just putting some champagne on ice for us and then he'll be off for the weekend. Won't you Perkins?

PERKINS: Definitely sir.

(Picks up tray and exits to kitchen. HARRY follows him to the kitchen door then turns to MARIAN.)

HARRY & MARIAN: *(Together)* Darling.

(They run together and kiss.)

HARRY: *(They break off slightly. HARRY holds her hands and looks down the front of her dress)* It's so nice to see you out again!

MARIAN: *(Breaks away R., and looks at the kitchen door)* I don't feel comfortable with him around.

HARRY: *(Reaching for her)* He'll be gone in a minute.

MARIAN: *(Side stepping around the sofa, to avoid HARRY's clutching hands)* Harry, you said we could draw up a plan for the whole evening this time with just the two of us.

HARRY: *(Gazing wistfully at her chest)* A whole evening with just the two of them – two of us I mean.

(He grabs for her again.)

MARIAN: *(Slips away)* Harry. Sex isn't everything you know.

HARRY: If that's what you think, then you're not doing it right!

MARIAN: Let's not rush things, we have a plan for this evening.

HARRY: You mean –

MARIAN: Yes. You said we could act out our fantasies, don't you remember?

HARRY: You mean you actually bought the costumes?

MARIAN: Of course, I've got yours right here.

(She puts the package on the chair.)

HARRY: *(Drooling a a little)* You mean you're actually going to dress up as a French maid?

MARIAN: Yes, but remember, we both agreed, so you're going to have to wear your costume as well.

HARRY: No problem! However, I think I'd better make absolutely certain Perkins has gone for the night. *(He goes to the kitchen door, opens it and looks in)* All clear, he's gone. *(Advances on MARIAN again)* Let the games begin.

MARIAN: *(Gently pushing him away)* Down Tiger! I'll tell you what. I'll pop home through the garden and get changed into my costume. You get the champagne ready, get into your costume and we'll meet back here in ten minutes.

(She moves to the French windows.)

HARRY: I can't wait my love.

MARIAN: *(Strikes a provocative pose and in a French accent)* Do not pour ze champagne, your personal maid will do that for you. *(Blows him a kiss)* Oo-la-la.

(Exits French windows.)

HARRY: *(Almost beside himself)* Oo-la-la.

(He exits to the kitchen singing, and returns immediately with a bottle of champagne in an ice-bucket and two glasses which he places on the coffee table and still singing exits to BR1.)

(The front door opens. Enter DEBBIE. She looks around, peers into the kitchen then goes back to the front door.)

DEBBIE: Come in Joe, it's O.K. They've all gone.

(Enter JOE. Young, clean cut, a little shy and nervous. He is wearing a conservative dark business suit and tie, and carrying a small overnight bag.)

JOE: Are you sure?

DEBBIE: Relax darling, we have the entire house to ourselves for the whole weekend.

(She kisses him.)

JOE: Are you sure nothing can go wrong?

DEBBIE: *(Closes the front door and propels JOE to the sofa)* Don't worry. Dad's playing golf in Scotland and Mom's locked up on a fat farm.

JOE: *(Sitting R. end of the sofa and relaxing a little)* It's just that I get a bit nervous thinking about your father. I've never met an ambassador before.

DEBBIE: *(Sits to JOE's L.)* Well you're not going to meet one now. *(Notices the champagne)* Well! Would you look at that! That Perkins is absolutely incredible.

JOE: Who's Perkins?

DEBBIE: Daddy's new butler. I was a bit worried about him but I sort of "dropped a hint" about us this weekend, and look what the old dear did. He opened some champagne and left it for us.

(She pours two glasses.)

JOE: You told him about us?

DEBBIE: Well, not in as many words, but he obviously got the message. I'm beginning to understand what Daddy meant when he said an English butler would add a touch of class. *(She hands JOE his glass)* Here's to a wonderful weekend.

(They drink.)

JOE: You know, I'm really looking forward to relaxing this weekend. I'm afraid it's been rather a rough week at the office.

DEBBIE: Busy huh?

JOE: You have no idea. This week it seemed like everyone wanted to go on vacation at the same time.

DEBBIE: Still, being a travel agent has its advantages. Think of all those free trips you get.

JOE: You know, all everyone ever thinks about travel agents are the free trips. There's a lot of work involved.

DEBBIE: I know dear, but let's not talk about work. *(She raises her glass)* Here's to the two of us, alone together, for a wild and wonderful weekend.

JOE: I'll drink to that. *(They drink, DEBBIE puts her glass down, takes JOE's glass from him and puts it down. She looks at him for a second, then leaps at him. They kiss)* I think I'd like to slip into something more comfortable.

DEBBIE: That's my line. *(They laugh and kiss briefly again)* O.K. come on. *(Getting up)* We'll be in my room. You can change and then we'll see if there's anything to eat.

(DEBBIE leaves her empty glass on the coffee table. JOE takes a half full glass with him, picks up his bag, they go arm in arm and exit to BR2.)

(HARRY, now minus his shirt and trousers and wearing white boxer shorts with red hearts all over them, enters from BR1 looking for the package MARIAN brought. He sees it on the chair and as he reaches for it, he notices there is only one champagne glass. He picks up the one glass, frowns, puts it down, goes into the kitchen and returns immediately with another glass which he puts on the table. He picks up the package and exits BR1.)

(DEBBIE comes out of BR2, crosses to the coffee table, refills her glass with champagne, and taking it with her, exits BR2.)

(HARRY comes out of BR1, crosses to the kitchen, goes in and returns immediately with a jar of caviar and some crackers on a plate which he puts on the coffee table. He notices there is only one glass. He gives a little strangled cry, picks up the remaining one, looks at it, looks under the table, scratches his head, puts down the glass, shrugs and returns to the kitchen.)

(DEBBIE comes out of BR2 and heads L. to the kitchen. She gets just past the coffee table when she stops and notices the caviar. She picks up the jar and one cracker, which she dips into the caviar as she returns to BR2 leaving only the plate with the rest of the crackers.)

(HARRY comes out of the kitchen with yet another champagne glass and puts it on the table. He notices the jar of caviar is gone and with a cry of anguish, looks around, throws his hands in the air and returns to the kitchen.)

(DEBBIE comes out of BR2 with the jar of caviar, puts it back on the table, dips another cracker in it and exits to the study.)

(HARRY comes out of the kitchen with another jar of caviar, sees one already on the table, gives a long loud moan, shakes his head and slowly returns to the kitchen.)

(DEBBIE comes out of the study carrying a pillow, crosses R., exits BR2.)

(HARRY darts out of the kitchen to the coffee table, expecting some change. There is none. He exits BR1 and closes the door. After two seconds he flings open the door, looks around, sees nothing and returns to BR1.)

(Enter DEBBIE and JOE from BR2. Both carrying champagne glasses. JOE is now wearing slacks and a sport shirt.)

DEBBIE: Don't you just love that champagne? Want some more?

JOE: Why not?

(They both move to the sofa.)

DEBBIE: *(Pouring champagne)* Oh, this is the life. You know I can't get over Perkins getting all this ready for us.

JOE: He doesn't sound like the usual English butler at all. What exactly did you say to him?

DEBBIE: Well, nothing much really. I just told him you'd be here, and he sort of looked disapprovingly at me and said he would be *(English accent)* "The absolute soul of discretion."

JOE: *(Raising his glass)* Well, if this is the touch of class, I'm all for it. Makes you feel a bit wicked though doesn't it?

DEBBIE: *(Laughing)* Wicked?

JOE: Well – French champagne and Russian caviar, it is a bit decadent don't you think?

DEBBIE: *(Snuggling closer and in a Russian accent)* "Drink ze champagne Boris so I can have my way with you."

JOE: I want you to know, I'm not a pushover –

DEBBIE: *(Feigning disappointment)* Oh dear!

JOE: But I can be had! If you play your cards right. *(They both laugh)* You know, my mother always said I'd end up with some girl getting me into trouble.

DEBBIE: *(Grabs him)* Here comes trouble!

(They kiss briefly.)

JOE: Talking about mothers, where did you say yours was?

DEBBIE: She's gone to a spa for the weekend.

JOE: That's not what you called it.

DEBBIE: I know, I called it a fat farm, but they're really in the moving business.

JOE: Now you lost me.

DEBBIE: It's very simple really. They remove surplus fat, wrinkles and hair from your body and then they move money from your pocket to theirs.

(They both laugh.)

JOE: You know it's not your mother that worries me, it's your father.

DEBBIE: What do you mean?

JOE: Well the fact that he's an ambassador absolutely terrifies me. I mean, I see his picture in the paper all the time. He's quite famous, and I've never met anyone famous like that. What's he like?

DEBBIE: Oh, he's a big pussycat! He's a sweetheart really, it's just that he's terribly old-fashioned with really quaint ideas on marriage and morality.

JOE: Such as?

DEBBIE: Well, he once referred to Queen Victoria as a loose woman!

JOE: Be serious.

DEBBIE: O.K. for example, if he knew about us this weekend, he'd have a heart attack.

JOE: Really?

DEBBIE: Yes, but only after horse-whipping you and disowning me.

JOE: I'm sure you make him sound worse than he really is.

DEBBIE: Probably, but he's such a puritan. *(She gets up)* I'll tell you what. Why don't we just put our things away and then get supper ready together in the kitchen.

JOE: *(Getting up as they both exit BR2, each with their champagne glass)* Well, I'm not much of a cook, but if you show me what to do I'll give it my best shot.

(Enter HARRY from BR1. He is now wearing nothing but a leopard skin Tarzan outfit. He strikes a pose in front of the mirror.)

(Enter PERKINS from the kitchen. He stands motionless in the doorway. HARRY, his back towards PERKINS, continues various poses and a feeble attempt at a Tarzan yell whilst beating his chest. Eventually PERKINS clears his throat.)

PERKINS: Ahem!

(HARRY jumps, turns, sees PERKINS and looks around for cover. He sees the raincoat by the front door, and taking giant strides, stands behind it. During the following conversation HARRY manages to get nonchalantly into the raincoat after grappling with the coat stand.)

HARRY: I thought you'd gone for the weekend.
PERKINS: Obviously sir!
HARRY: Now look here Perkins –
PERKINS: I'd really rather not sir.
HARRY: Not what?
PERKINS: Look.
HARRY: What I mean is –

PERKINS: Are we going to have our soul of discretion conversation again?

HARRY: I think that might well be a very good idea.

PERKINS: Can we go right to "not a word to you know who"?

HARRY: Excellent!

PERKINS: *(Aside)* No one would believe me anyway.

(The door to BR2 opens and DEBBIE comes out followed by JOE.)

DEBBIE: Come on, it'll be such fun, we can both cook dinner together –

(She sees PERKINS and HARRY and quickly pushes JOE back into the bedroom behind her.)

HARRY: Good heavens Debbie! What are you doing here?

DEBBIE: I – er – decided to stay home after all.

HARRY: Who's that you were talking to?

DEBBIE: Aren't you in Scotland?

HARRY: No – no – the – er – weather forecast wasn't good. *(Pause)* You didn't answer my question.

DEBBIE: What question was that?

HARRY: Who's that you were talking to in your room?

DEBBIE: Talking? In my room? Er – it's Joe – *(Struck with a brilliant idea)* er – Josephine. It's my girlfriend Josephine.

HARRY: Well, aren't you going to bring her out and introduce us?

DEBBIE: No.

HARRY: What?

DEBBIE: She's – er – changing, she'll be out in a few minutes.

MARIAN: *(Comes through the French windows now wearing the stereotype French maid's outfit. Short black skirt, white apron, black fish net stockings, high heels, etc.)* Oo-la-la! *(Sees everyone)* Oo-la-la.

DEBBIE: *(After a long pause)* Daddy? Who is this?

HARRY: *(Looks around for help, none is forthcoming. PERKINS rolls his eyes heavenward)* This is our new maid, Marian.

MARIAN: Maid?

PERKINS: And you wanted me to go to London. I wouldn't miss this for the world.

HARRY: *(Now regaining his composure)* Yes. We said we were getting a maid, don't you remember Perkins? Perhaps you should take her into the kitchen and show her the ropes.

PERKINS: I would have thought you would be more suitably dressed to show her ropes sir!

HARRY: Perkins!

PERKINS: Yes sir. This way miss.

(He holds open the kitchen door. MARIAN mouths something unintelligible at HARRY as she passes him, and she and PERKINS exit to the kitchen.)

HARRY: Now my dear, I'll just get dressed and then you can introduce me to your girl friend.

(Exits BR1.)

DEBBIE: *(Goes into BR2 leaving the door open) (Off)* Quick, put this on.

JOE: *(Off)* No, no, I'm not going to wear a dress.

DEBBIE: *(Off)* Come on.

JOE: *(Off)* I tell you I won't do it.

DEBBIE: *(Crossing to the study in a great hurry)* It's just for a little while, till I figure out how to get us out of here.

(Goes into the study.)

JOE: *(Off)* There's no way I'm putting this on. It's too small anyway. Oh, this is ridiculous. It simply doesn't fit. Debbie this is the stupidest thing you've ever asked me to do –

DEBBIE: *(Returning from the study with a lady's wig on a small stand)* We'll just introduce you to Daddy, he'll never know the difference.

(Exit BR2.)

JOE: *(Off, as DEBBIE closes the door)* No – No – No!

(The door bell rings. PERKINS comes out of the kitchen and opens it to reveal CAPTAIN SOUTH. He is a U.S. Marine Corps Officer, in uniform. He will be followed by the ambassador's secretary, FAYE. She is young, blonde, full figured and clearly has not become HARRY's secretary by reason of her office skills. She is wearing a white long sleeve blouse with ruffles, a black pencil skirt, high heels and has a purse over one shoulder. She carries a red telephone and a computer keyboard piled high with file folders, papers, etc.)

SOUTH: *(Strides past PERKINS, who is holding the door and makes an inspection of the room, moving from the French windows to the doors of BR1 and BR2 while talking)* My name is South, Captain South, United States Marine Corps. I'm in charge of security at the embassy. There's been a bomb threat at the embassy and plan "M" is now in effect.

PERKINS: Plan "M"?

SOUTH: Plan "M". The embassy has been evacuated. This house is now the temporary embassy. *(FAYE appears in the open front door)* This is Miss Baker, the ambassador's secretary.

PERKINS: *(To FAYE, who is standing still, loaded down)* How do you do? *(FAYE tries to free a hand to shake hands, papers fall)* May I help you miss?

FAYE: Oh, thank you. *(She tries to hand PERKINS the keyboard and most of the remaining papers fall)* Oh dear. *(She puts the phone and her purse on the desk and starts to pick up the papers)* There they go again.

PERKINS: *(Has put the keyboard on the desk and helps her pick up the papers)* Never mind, miss, we'll have them all straightened out in a minute.

SOUTH: *(Pressing right on)* Miss Baker, set up communications please. *(FAYE looks blankly at him)* Plug in the phone!

(FAYE plugs in the red phone. In so doing she manages to knock her purse and several other papers on to the floor. She picks them up again.)

PERKINS: Excuse me, but what exactly is this Plan "M"?

SOUTH: This house is now completely sealed off. A squad of marines is in the grounds and no-one will be permitted in or out. The red telephone you see here has a built in scrambler, and Miss Baker will now make sure we are in contact with the State Department in Washington. *(FAYE looks blank. Pause)* Won't you Miss Baker.

FAYE: Won't I what?

SOUTH: Make contact with the State Department.

FAYE: Oh yes, if you'd like me to.

SOUTH: I should definitely like you to.

FAYE: O.K.

(She does nothing.)

SOUTH: Now please, Miss Baker!

FAYE: Oh, you mean you want me to dial that number you gave me?

SOUTH: I think we've finally struck grey matter.

PERKINS: *(Kindly)* I think he wants you to call Washington.

FAYE: Well, why didn't he say so?

(She dials.)

SOUTH: *(Turning his attention to PERKINS)* Now, who the devil are you, and where is the ambassador?

PERKINS: I'm Perkins. I'm the butler, and I have no idea where Mr. Douglas is. Probably climbing a tree with Jane!

SOUTH: I beg your pardon.

PERKINS: I said I don't know when I'll see him again.

SOUTH: *(To FAYE, who has now put the phone down)* Everything O.K.? *(FAYE nods)* Good. Now why don't you get the rest of your equipment. I'm going to check the left flank.

PERKINS: The what?

SOUTH: The garden.

(He exits French windows. FAYE exits front door, closing it. PERKINS exits kitchen.)

(Enter DEBBIE and JOE from BR2. JOE is now dressed as a woman in wig, dress, makeup, etc.)

JOE: He'll never believe I'm a girl.

DEBBIE: Of course he will, just don't say too much.

JOE: This is ridiculous.

DEBBIE: I'll just introduce you. Daddy will be satisfied and then we'll both get out of here for the weekend. Now, go get a drink or something while I put your clothes in a suitcase.

(Exit BR2.)

(JOE crosses L. to the credenza.)

HARRY: *(Enters from BR1, now in slacks and shirt)* What the devil's all the noise about? *(Sees JOE)* Oh, hello. You must be Debbie's friend Josephine?

JOE: *(At the credenza. In a high voice)* Yes, hello.

HARRY: *(Crosses L. with outstretched arm to shake hands. When he gets there, instead of shaking JOE's offered hand, he picks it up and kisses it)* Hello, beautiful!

JOE: *(Backing hurriedly away)* How do you do Mr. Douglas?

HARRY: *(Advancing lustfully)* I'm very well thank you. Now that I've met you.

JOE: *(Breaks away and dodges down stage across R. in front of the sofa)* Yes – well – *(He is now close to BR2)* DEBBIE *(This word almost in a scream)* and I are just going out.

HARRY: *(Continues to move around the sofa. JOE continues to back away)* Why don't you stay for a while? We could get to know each other. I could probably surprise you with a thing or two.

JOE: I could probably surprise you with a thing or two.

HARRY: I'll bet we could make the earth move.

JOE: I take it you mean without the benefit of a bulldozer.

HARRY: You got it.

JOE: Maybe the earth moved ten million years ago when the dinosaurs were jumping on each other, but not tonight.

HARRY: And why not tonight Josephine?

(Advancing rapidly he succeeds in pinching JOE's derriere.)

JOE: *(Normal voice)* Mr. Douglas! *(High voice)* I mean Mr. Douglas! You're a married man.

(Backing away.)

HARRY: *(Still advancing)* Yes, but polygamy was always better than monotony.

JOE: Believe me, I'm just not your type.

(He finally runs out of the French windows pursued by HARRY.)

(Enter FAYE through the front door, overburdened with computer console, folders, papers, etc. She knocks over the coat stand. Puts the computer on the desk and goes back to pick up the coat stand. Now drops papers all over the floor, falls over the coat stand, etc. She finally gets back to the desk and sits down.)

MARIAN: *(Enters from the kitchen)* Oh, hello.

(She goes R. to just above the chair.)

FAYE: Hello *(Pause)* You must be the maid.

MARIAN: No – that is yes – that is maybe – who are you?

FAYE: *(Stands up)* I'm Faye Baker, Mr. Douglas' secretary.

MARIAN: Hi. *(Looking her up and down)* His secretary eh? Well you're a lucky girl. How do you keep that figure sitting at a desk all day?

FAYE: Well, I used to have this exercise program running six miles a day, but I got so tired, I'd have to take a taxi back to my apartment, and it got too expensive.

MARIAN: *(Pause)* I see. *(Pause)* You can type can you?

FAYE: Type what?

MARIAN: You know – letters.

FAYE: Oh yes. *(Pause)* Some of them anyway.

MARIAN: Perhaps you'd better tell me what you're doing here.

FAYE: They've closed the embassy. There's a mad bomber or something, so we have to work here.

MARIAN: On a Friday night?

FAYE: Well, someone has to stay in contact with Washington and it's my turn this weekend.

MARIAN: You're going to stay all weekend?

FAYE: Probably, they have to get the bomb squad to search the whole building. It takes forever.

MARIAN: Well, this is the end. Where's Harry?

FAYE: I really don't know.

MARIAN: Well, you're his secretary – give him a message. *(FAYE drops the papers she is holding, searches for and eventually finds a steno pad and pencil while MARIAN waits)* Tell him, I've *(Pause)* gone *(Pause)* home.

(She storms across the room and exits French windows.)
(Enter SOUTH and HARRY through the front door.)

SOUTH: So you see sir, we have the place completely sealed off. No one in – no one out. Ah, Miss Baker, getting things straight I see.

HARRY: But I don't want a bunch of marines running around the place.

SOUTH: Sorry, sir. You know the regulations when Plan "M" is in effect. Now I'll leave you two to get *(He pauses and looks briefly at the mess on and around the desk)* organized while I check the perimeter.

(Exits front door.)

FAYE: *(Still moving things around the desk)* Is there anything you'd like me to do sir?

HARRY: *(Pacing around)* Well, no, not really. Is there anything in the "Urgent" folder? *(FAYE shuffles papers, finds the "Urgent" folder, takes out a pen and writes something on it)* What are you doing?

FAYE: I'm writing your name on this folder.

HARRY: Why?

FAYE: Because; it's for you.

HARRY: *(Rolling his eyes heavenward)* Why don't you put my address on it, and my phone number, and then write "folder" on the outside, so anyone who comes near it will know what it is?

FAYE: *(Starts to write again)* Yes, sir.

HARRY: The day I find a retarded chimp, you're fired.

FAYE: I know. There was something. Someone came to see you.

HARRY: Who?

FAYE: I've forgotten.

HARRY: Well, was it a man or a woman?

FAYE: *(Thoughtful)* Yes!

HARRY: *(Tearing at his hair)* What was it about?

FAYE: About 2:30 I guess.

HARRY: *(Placing his hands round an imaginary neck)* No jury in the world would convict me. *(Pause)* I give up.

FAYE: I'm sorry Mr. Douglas, you always get me so flustered.

HARRY: I know, I know. I'm just trying to raise your consciousness a little. *(Aside)* Providing, that is, you are conscious. *(Looking around)* By the way, have you seen Miss Murdoch?

FAYE: Who?

HARRY: The maid. Marian.

FAYE: Yes, she left you a message.

HARRY: I'm almost afraid to ask. Yes?

FAYE: *(Looks for and eventually finds her steno pad)* She went home.

HARRY: Oh no! *(Exit hurriedly through French windows)* Marian, Marian.

(Enter PERKINS from the kitchen with a tray. He comes D. to the coffee table, picks up the glasses and champagne bottle then places them on the credenza.)

PERKINS: Have you got everything you need miss?

FAYE: *(Dabbing her eyes with handkerchief)* Yes, I think so. Thank you.

PERKINS: Are you alright miss?

FAYE: *(With a little sob)* I guess so.

PERKINS: *(Coming back L. and takes her hands in his)* Something is wrong isn't it?

FAYE: *(Stands up)* I shouldn't let it upset me. I should be used to him by now.

PERKINS: Used to whom?

FAYE: Mr. Douglas.

PERKINS: Oh, I see. No I don't see. What are we talking about?

FAYE: He's always making comments about me. I pretend not to notice, but I know he thinks I'm kind of dumb.

PERKINS: Oh no, I'm sure you're quite wrong.

FAYE: No, it's true. I can tell.

PERKINS: What sort of comments?

FAYE: Well, yesterday he yelled at me just because I thought the Gettysburg Address was where Lincoln lived.

PERKINS: Oh dear!

FAYE: Then he said my intellect underwhelmed him.

PERKINS: Oh dear!

FAYE: Then he suggested I hold a seance to see if it was possible to make contact with my brain.

PERKINS: I see. That's not very nice is it? Why don't you come in the kitchen. I'll make you a nice cup of tea.

FAYE: Thank you, that would be nice. *(She reaches to pick up her purse from the desk and knocks the vase over behind it)* Oh dear, I've done it again. *(Holds up the vase, now in two pieces)* Never mind, it won't take a minute.

(She gets busy sorting through her purse.)

PERKINS: *(Puzzled)* What are you doing?

FAYE: Here it is.

(Holds up a small plastic tube.)

PERKINS: What's that?

FAYE: This is the modern miracle of twentieth century science. The one thing a girl like me should never be without.

PERKINS: What is it?

FAYE: Super duper wonder glue.

PERKINS: *(Incredulous)* What?

FAYE: Super duper wonder glue.

PERKINS: You carry your own tube of super glue?

FAYE: Oh yes, I don't leave home without it. I go through a tube about every two weeks. Here hold this. *(She hands PERKINS the vase)* It's real easy.

(She unscrews the cap and applies glue to the vase.)

PERKINS: Oh – oh – oh. Steady on. You've got it all over my hand.

(Holds up his right hand.)

FAYE: Oh dear, that's bad. Don't touch anything for a minute.

PERKINS: What gets it off?

FAYE: I don't know. I've only ever put it on. Wait a minute while I put this down. *(She puts down the vase and glue. She comes R. behind PERKINS to see his right hand)* Now, let me see. Oh dear.

(They are now standing just upstage and slightly to the R, of the desk. PERKINS holds his right hand down, palm forwards.)

SOUTH: *(Enters from the kitchen on the dead run. He has a walkie-talkie held to his ear)* What do you mean there's a maid on the fence?

(As he rushes past, PERKINS turns R.U.S. to see who it is. SOUTH knocks PERKINS' right hand against FAYE's derriere, and exits through the French windows.)

(PERKINS moves his right hand as FAYE looks at him in disbelief. Eventually giving up the struggle to free his hand, PERKINS stands very still facing D.S. and not looking at FAYE, who is also now standing stock still.)

FAYE: *(Eventually)* Mr. Perkins.

PERKINS: *(Trying to be nonchalant)* Yes, my dear?

FAYE: Your hand.

PERKINS: Yes, I know.

FAYE: I'd like you to remove it please.

PERKINS: I don't believe that's possible.

FAYE: You mean the super duper wonder glue?

PERKINS: I mean the super duper wonder glue.

(PERKINS tries yet again to free his hand, accompanied by giggles and wiggles from FAYE.)

FAYE: *(Giggling)* I think maybe you should hold still.

PERKINS: I was merely trying to secure the release of my hand.

FAYE: Here try this.

(She wiggles her hips, but all that happens is the skirt rides up from the bottom leaving PERKINS' hand firmly in place.)

PERKINS: *(Looking around and trying hard not to look at her now revealed lingerie)* I think perhaps it might be better if you pulled it down. *(She wiggles again and gets the skirt back to normal)* Oh dear, this is most embarrassing. I can't be seen like this.

(Enter MARIAN and HARRY through the French windows followed by SOUTH.)

MARIAN: What do you mean, I can't go home?

HARRY: I'm sorry but its plan "M".

(They all stop, stand still and look at PERKINS' hand.)

PERKINS: *(After a moment's pause during which he looks down at his hand then grins at HARRY, he takes FAYE's right hand in his left and starts to tango around the room. They dance around the room and then straight through the kitchen door, without breaking stride, as PERKINS calls out the beat)* Rum – pum – pum – ta – da – da – dada.

HARRY: *(Quietly)* Perkins *(Pause, louder)* PERKINS!

PERKINS: *(Opens the kitchen door and steps into the living room. They are now back to back. FAYE is still stuck right next to him to his left. Her derriere towards the living room)* Yes sir?

HARRY: What were you doing with my secretary?

PERKINS: Your secretary sir?

HARRY: My secretary, Miss Baker.

PERKINS: Ah yes, Miss Baker. I was teaching her to dance.

HARRY: May I be so bold as to ask why?

PERKINS: Well, the fact is sir, she was helping me.

HARRY: And why do you need my secretary's help?

PERKINS: I've only been here two weeks sir, and I'm still – *(He looks at his right hand as FAYE gives a wiggle)* – feeling my way around! And in any event I'd got a little behind in my work.

(FAYE wiggles again.)

HARRY: A little behind in your work?

PERKINS: Yes sir. The fact is, right now, I seem to have my hands full.

HARRY: Nonsense.

MARIAN: Harry – do something.

HARRY: I'm trying to dear, I'm trying. Perkins, go make some sandwiches, it looks like a long evening.

PERKINS: Very good sir.

(They return to the kitchen, FAYE still facing L. and PERKINS shuffling backwards.)

SOUTH: Perhaps sir, it might be a good idea if you explained this lady's presence.

HARRY: She's the new maid.

SOUTH: Do you have an explanation as to why I found her in a gap in the garden fence trying to break in here?

MARIAN: I was trying to break out, not in, you dimwit.

HARRY: Now, now, dear –

MARIAN: Harry, don't you think it is about time –

HARRY: Why don't you go in the bedroom and turn down the bed? *(He ushers her towards BR1)* I'll be along in a minute.

(Exit MARIAN BR1.)

SOUTH: Is there anyone else I haven't seen yet?

HARRY: Well, there's my daughter Debbie, whom you know, and her girl-friend Josephine.

SOUTH: Do you know where they are sir?

HARRY: They're around here somewhere.

SOUTH: You're sure there's no-one else?

HARRY: Quite sure.

(The red phone rings, before HARRY or SOUTH can react, FAYE opens the kitchen door and steps into the living

room to answer it. PERKINS, his hand still in place "snuggles up" behind her.)

FAYE: United States Embassy, Ambassador Douglas' office – good – thank you. *(She hangs up then moves R. towards HARRY. PERKINS is pulled with her)* They're just testing the line sir.

HARRY: Why are you hanging around my secretary all the time Perkins?

PERKINS: Well – we've formed quite a bond between us sir.

HARRY: *(Eyes heavenward)* Get the sandwiches Perkins.

PERKINS: Yes sir. *(He looks round for a way to escape to the kitchen)* Conga! *(He takes FAYE's left hand in his left hand and they Conga to the kitchen, his right hand still on her derriere as PERKINS calls out the beat)* Ra – ta – ta – ta – tata!

HARRY: Now. *(Rubbing his hands together in anticipation)* I think I'll just go and supervise the maid. If you need me, I'll be in there.

(Indicates and then exits to BR1.)
(SOUTH heads for the kitchen.)

DEBBIE: *(Comes out of BR2, sees SOUTH)* Oh! *(SOUTH stops and turns as FAYE/PERKINS come out of the kitchen. SOUTH is hit by the door. The kitchen door swings slowly closed. SOUTH stands upright for a moment, then falls unconscious to the floor) (Crossing L)* Is he hurt?

FAYE: Oh dear, I've done it again!

PERKINS: I must say my dear, you have been rather rotten to the corps!

DEBBIE: We'd better put him on the couch. *(FAYE and PERKINS manage to conceal his hand still stuck to her. DEBBIE takes SOUTH's legs L., FAYE and PERKINS takes his head and shoulders R. They just get him on the couch when his trousers are pulled down revealing his undershorts which have a U.S. flag sewn across the seat. They all salute and pause in their labors)* What sort of shorts are they?

PERKINS: I believe they're called boxer shorts miss.

FAYE: I've always liked jockey shorts myself.

DEBBIE: That's funny, I wonder why they call them jockey shorts?

FAYE: *(Giggles)* I always thought it was something to do with – "They're off".

PERKINS: Ahem!

DEBBIE: I think he'll be alright in a minute. By the way Miss Baker, what are you doing here?

FAYE: There's been a bomb threat at the embassy, we all have to stay and work here.

DEBBIE: Oh dear, I wonder where Joe is.

PERKINS: Who?

DEBBIE: I mean has anyone seen my girl friend Josephine?

PERKINS: I believe I saw her in the garden miss.

DEBBIE: Thank you, Perkins.

(Exits French windows.)

FAYE: Last week he was unconscious for nearly half an hour.

PERKINS: Good heavens. What happened last week?

FAYE: It was an accident really, but I hit him with a fax machine.

PERKINS: You know, I don't want you to take this the wrong way, but I really do think you are going to have to take your skirt off.

FAYE: What am I going to wear?

PERKINS: I'm not sure but we can't go on forever like this.

FAYE: Oh I don't mind really, I'm beginning to get quite used to it.

(She giggles.)

PERKINS: Yes, I know what you mean. *(He sighs)* But you have things to do and I have sandwiches to make. Have you ever tried to make sandwiches with one hand?

FAYE: O.K. but you're going to have to find me another skirt.

PERKINS: Of course I will. I'll ask Miss Deborah as soon as she gets back.

FAYE: Well, alright then.

(She unfastens her skirt and steps out of it as JOE and DEBBIE come through the French windows. JOE is totally disheveled, his wig a little crooked and bits of shrubbery hanging all over.)

DEBBIE: *(Laughing)* Well Perkins, is this what the butler saw?

PERKINS: *(Flustered and holding the skirt behind his back)* Now miss – it's not at all what you think.

DEBBIE: *(Enjoying this)* And what do you think I think, Perkins?

PERKINS: Really, miss, this is too much, would you kindly lend me a skirt please?

JOE: No one is going to believe me when I tell them what is going on around here.

DEBBIE: There's nothing going on around here.

JOE: *(Takes DEBBIE's arm and leads her D.S.L. away from PERKINS and FAYE)* No? I'm standing here, wearing a dress, there's a half dressed blonde who's giggling at your butler, who has just asked to borrow a skirt. Sleeping beauty here on the couch is showing the flag. I haven't even told you about the Ambassador yet, and you say there's nothing going on?

DEBBIE: Now don't get excited.

JOE: I shall not get excited. I shall go into the bedroom. I shall change clothes and Debbie, we shall then both leave this madhouse.

(Exits BR2.)

DEBBIE: He – er – she'll be alright. I'll find you a skirt, won't be a second.

(Exits BR2, leaving the door open.)

PERKINS: Perhaps you might feel more comfortable if you wait in the study.

FAYE: Thank you, I will.

PERKINS: *(They cross L. together)* If you need anything just let me know, I'll be in the kitchen.

FAYE: Thank you, Perkins.

(PERKINS opens the study door, FAYE exits.)

PERKINS: *(To the door of BR2)* I'm in the kitchen Miss Deborah.

DEBBIE: *(Off)* O.K.

(PERKINS exits to kitchen.)

SOUTH: *(Groaning and feeling his head)* Ooooh my head. *(Waking up)* The bomber! He's here. *(He hitches up his pants and goes to the front door to listen)* Ah – ha! *(He listens at the kitchen door)* Ah – ha! *(He listens at the study door)* Ah – ha!

(FAYE opens the study door, flattens him against the wall and exits to the kitchen.)

FAYE: I'd rather wait here with you Perkins.

(The study door slowly swings away from the wall, revealing SOUTH who crumples ever so slowly to the floor.)

DEBBIE: *(Comes out of BR2 with a skirt in her hand and crosses to the kitchen. She opens the door and leans in)* Here you are Perkins.

(She hands the skirt through the door and returns to BR2.)

SOUTH: *(Rising slowly and groaning)* We're under attack. I must get reinforcements.

(He staggers out of the French windows, leaving them open.)

DEBBIE: *(Coming out of BR2, putting on a windbreaker)* Alright darling, we'll go. Just don't yell at me. Put on your clothes and we'll get out of here. *(She struggles with the zipper)* Damn! *(Enter PERKINS from the kitchen. He is now minus the vest, his sleeves rolled up and wearing a small white bartender type apron, his tie hanging loose)* Perkins, would you give me a hand with this zipper please, it's stuck.

PERKINS: Certainly miss. *(He crosses R. to DEBBIE who is just L. of the door of BR2. He struggles with the zipper)* It's really stuck miss. *(He finally gets it to move, but his tie is firmly caught in it)* Oh my goodness. *(His head is now firmly wedged in the center of DEBBIE's chest)* My tie appears to be stuck miss. Could you please do something, I can hardly breathe.

DEBBIE: I'm trying. *(She struggles with the zipper. She turns as best she can and calls over her right shoulder into BR2)* Joe, would you help us please?

JOE: *(Now minus wig and dress, wearing a shirt, undershorts and holding a pair of trousers into which he has just put one leg, appears hopping in the doorway)* Yeah?

DEBBIE: We're a bit stuck, give us a hand will you?

JOE: O.K. *(He puts his other leg in the trousers and goes to move around them downstage. As he lets go of his trousers to help, they fall down. He pauses)* Just a second. *(Now standing very close behind DEBBIE and leaning on the door frame he zips up his trousers)* Ow! *(He is now firmly zipped to the rear of DEBBIE's dress. He has to remain on tip-toes or suffer the painful consequences. In a high voice)* Help!

DEBBIE: What is it?
JOE: My zipper is caught in your dress.
DEBBIE: *(Trying to turn)* Oh dear.
JOE: *(Yelling)* Don't move!
PERKINS: *(Muffled)* I'm suffocating.

(The white phone rings. PERKINS starts to shuffle backwards. DEBBIE shuffles forwards and JOE is forced to follow with a series of little shuffles each punctuated with:)

JOE: Ow – ow – ow – ow.

(Eventually they reach the phone which PERKINS picks up. He tries first one side and then the other, but is unable to get the phone in the right place as DEBBIE's chest is in the way. He finally hands the phone to her.)

DEBBIE: Hello, yes. Oh hi Margaret. Oh nothing much – sure – you're kidding – no – Margaret! Are you sure? Wait till everybody hears about this – she said what? *(PERKINS, his head buried, is frantically waving his arms. DEBBIE keeps shifting her position slightly and every movement causes JOE to wince and moan)* Oh Margaret, I don't believe it. It's too good to be true. Of course, I won't tell a soul. Well, no, actually I'm rather busy right now. I'm caught up in a number of things. O.K. Margaret. Thanks for calling.

(She hangs up.)

JOE: Who was that?

DEBBIE: *(Pauses and gives him an icy stare over her shoulder)* Never mind, we've got to get out of this mess.

PERKINS: Do you have any scissors miss?

DEBBIE: That's it. Yes, there's some in my room.

JOE: *(Looks at the door of BR2 and realizes they have to cross again)* Oh no! *(They now turn right around with PERKINS R., JOE L. and shuffle as before to BR2. Again JOE is forced to do his little jumps punctuated with:)* Ow – ow – ow – ow.

(They disappear into BR2 and re-appear immediately. PERKINS L., JOE R. and stop right outside the door to BR2. DEBBIE is holding a very large, wicked looking pair of scissors. She fumbles around PERKINS neck.)

DEBBIE: It's no good. I can't see.

PERKINS: Here, give them to me. *(She hands him the scissors)* Miss Deborah, would you hitch up your dress a little please?

(She does so and PERKINS reaches beneath her legs and snips the scissors menacingly.)

JOE: *(Screaming)* STOP! What are you going to do?

PERKINS: What do you think I'm going to do?

JOE: Not to me you're not.

DEBBIE: It'll be alright darling, just hold still.

JOE:*(Panic stricken)* What do you mean, it'll be alright? It's not you he's operating on.

PERKINS: *(Snipping the scissors)* If you hold very still, sir, I'm sure I can find the right place.

JOE: Ow! That was definitely not the right place.

PERKINS: Never mind, I think I've got it now sir.

JOE: Got what?

PERKINS: Now, just a little to the left, and up a fraction –

JOE: Don't talk about fractions.

PERKINS: I think I'm getting the hang of it now sir.

JOE: I don't want you to get the hang of anything.

PERKINS: I'm about ready sir.

JOE: *(Screaming)* STOP! I've heard of operating in the dark, but this is ridiculous.

PERKINS: I really thing we ought to get on with it before I run out of oxygen.

DEBBIE: Do be careful Perkins.

PERKINS: Ready?

DEBBIE: Ready!

JOE: Oh no!

PERKINS: Hup!

(DEBBIE gives a little jump to spread her feet wider. PERKINS cuts.)

JOE: OW! *(Screams and falls down)* Oh – Oh!

(Clutching the front of his trousers.)

(Enter HARRY and MARIAN from BR1. They both move to the rear of the sofa. They see PERKINS and DEBBIE, but not JOE, who is just out of sight by the door of BR2 and now on the floor.)

HARRY: Perkins! What are you doing to my daughter?

CURTAIN

ACT II

Scene One

(While the action is continuous, JOE will have changed into the "cut out" trousers and PERKINS to the "cut off" tie.)

HARRY: I'm beginning to have doubts about you Perkins. First my secretary and now my daughter.

PERKINS: *(His head still buried in DEBBIE's chest. Her skirt still hitched right up)* I can assure you, sir, this is none of my doing.

HARRY: No? It doesn't look like it.

PERKINS: I seem to have fallen into a booby trap sir!

HARRY: I don't know what you're doing to my daughter, and I don't even want to think about my secretary.

MARIAN: Your secretary?

HARRY: Yes, you know, the one with the big floppy discs!

PERKINS: Actually I found her intellectually quite stimulating.

HARRY: Her idea of intellectual stimulation is to count along with Big Bird! Now Debbie, perhaps you would care to explain just exactly what is going on here.

DEBBIE: There's nothing to explain really.

HARRY: *(Getting excited)* Nothing to explain? Perkins here has his hands – er – heaven knows where his hands are and his head is on your – er – your –

DEBBIE: Boobs!

HARRY: *(Cringing)* Don't use that word. I've told you that before.

DEBBIE: What word would you like me to use?

HARRY: Oh never mind. How did he get there?

DEBBIE: His tie is caught in my zipper.

HARRY: Well, I'll soon fix that ... *(Strides down stage)* Here, give me those scissors. *(He takes them from PERKINS and now sees JOE for the first time)* Who's this?

(He pushes PERKINS/DEBBIE L.)

DEBBIE: This is – er – er – Perkins' brother.

PERKINS: *(Lifts his head and starts to speak)* My what?

(DEBBIE shoves his head back down and all that is heard is totally unintelligible as DEBBIE keeps his head down in the depths of her chest.)

HARRY: *(Suspicious)* Oh, what's his name?

DEBBIE: *(Together)* Marc –

JOE: *(Together)* Anthony.

DEBBIE: Marc Anthony!

HARRY: *(In disbelief)* Marc Anthony?

DEBBIE: Marc Anthony.

HARRY: Perkins' brother?

DEBBIE: Perkins' brother.

HARRY: I don't suppose your first name is Brutus is it Perkins? *(Muffled noises from PERKINS. He shakes his head which starts DEBBIE's chest wobbling. DEBBIE puts her hands on his head to stop the motion, then gently pats the top of his head)* Well Mr. Marc Anthony Perkins, what are you doing on the floor? *(JOE stands up to reveal the front of his trousers completely cut away. He stands, trying to cover the gaping hole with his hands. JOE now puts one hand in his trousers pocket and from the inside makes a further unsuccessful attempt to cover the hole. The pocket too has been cut away and JOE's hand appears in the hole only to be quickly withdrawn)* Perhaps you would care to give me an explanation young man.

JOE: What explanation sir?

HARRY: Well, you must admit, it doesn't happen every day that I walk into my living room to find a relic of the Roman Empire, with half his pants missing, lying in the doorway of my daughter's bedroom!

JOE: Ah, yes. That explanation.

(PERKINS makes muffled noises.)

HARRY: Oh shut up! *(To JOE)* Yes – that explanation.

JOE: It's very simple really.

HARRY: *(Pause)* I'm waiting.

JOE: You tell him Debbie.

DEBBIE: Me? – er – you'd like to know why he's here and what happened to his trousers?

HARRY: Oh, indeed I would.

DEBBIE: MOTHS!

HARRY: What?

DEBBIE: Moths. Giant moths. He's had trouble with them for years.

HARRY: What?

DEBBIE: They ate his trousers. He's here to get a new pair from his brother.

PERKINS: *(Comes up for air. Muffled)* I say, could somebody do something?

MARIAN: He may be perfectly willing to die happy, but he is looking a little red around the ears.

HARRY: Here!

(He cuts and PERKINS straightens up, his tie is now cut off, close to the knot, and a big silly grin all over his face.)

PERKINS: Thank you. Now sir, about my brother.

DEBBIE: *(Grabs PERKINS and takes him downstage L)* Neither am I here to volunteer information to him about his family.

HARRY: Perkins may I suggest you get your brother some trousers.

DEBBIE: That's a good idea. Come along Perkins. *(She takes his arm)* We'll all go to your apartment and get some trousers for – er Marc Anthony, and we can all have a little talk.

PERKINS: I think that might be an excellent idea Miss Deborah.

(Exit front door, DEBBIE, JOE, PERKINS. JOE shuffling with his knees bent, still trying to cover up the hole.)

MARIAN: This place is a nut house. Now really Harry, I've gone along with everything, but you know, when you said you wanted me to dress up as a French maid, you didn't say anything about actually being one.

HARRY: Why don't you sit down and relax. *(He leads her to the couch, she sits L. side)* Let me get you a drink, my love, while I explain.

(Goes to credenza.)

MARIAN: You know, I really only put this outfit on so I could take it off!

HARRY: And so you shall my dear, and so you shall, but things have got rather complicated. You see, there's a bomb scare at the embassy and plan "M" is in effect. That means no-one can leave here.

MARIAN: Is that why Rambo out there stopped me going home?

HARRY: That's it exactly.

MARIAN: Well just how long does he intend to keep us all here?

HARRY: It's difficult to say really. It depends on how long the bomb squad takes to clear the embassy.

(Brings her drink.)

MARIAN: You mean we could be here all night?

HARRY: Yes, it's possible.

(Sits R. side of couch.)

(SOUTH appears in the French windows. He is now in combat boots and fatigues. He stops dead in his tracks as MARIAN speaks.)

MARIAN: Well, in that case I think we should give up the deception and tell everyone who I really am.

(SOUTH takes out pad and pencil and ducks almost out of sight.)

HARRY: We can't do that.

MARIAN: And why not?

HARRY: Well, in the first place, I don't want anyone to know who you are, especially that mad marine *(SOUTH reacts)* out there, and in the second place, there's no point, we'd still be stuck in here for the evening so we might as well continue with the original plan.

MARIAN: But there are all these people here.

HARRY: Sooner or later everyone is going to leave and go to bed and I'll work it so we can be alone.

MARIAN: How are we going to be alone with half the U.S. Marine Corps running around out there?

HARRY: You leave that to me. I can handle that young dropout from the halls of Montezuma.

(SOUTH reacts.)

MARIAN: I must admit, Harry, you make some pretty fast moves. Do you remember when I was nearly caught behind the curtain?

(SOUTH reacts to the word "curtain" carefully writing it down.)

HARRY: *(Laughing)* I don't think I'll ever forget it, and then we had to get you out over the wall.

(SOUTH reacts to the word "wall" carefully writing it down.)

MARIAN: Oh Harry, you're so clever. I don't know how you get away with it. One of these days you're going to get caught you know.

HARRY: As long as I don't get caught with my trousers down, eh?

MARIAN: That depends on who's doing the catching.

(SOUTH ducks out of sight as HARRY laughs, gets up, and moves slowly and suggestively toward the door of BR1. He beckons with his finger.)

HARRY: Let's see if you can catch me then.

MARIAN: *(Gets up and moves sensually towards HARRY)* Ooh, la, la.

HARRY: *(Opens the bedroom door as MARIAN enters)* Here comes the lean, mean ambassadorial machine.

(Exit BR1 and closes door.)

(SOUTH enters from the French windows and strides purposefully across to the kitchen. He opens the door and calls.)

SOUTH: Miss Baker. *(FAYE enters)* We have a most serious development. *(Striding back and forth across the room)* Patch in direct to the Central Intelligence Agency. *(FAYE sits at the desk)* Now. *(Slight pause)* C.I.A. Langley, Virginia, U.S.A. Request information concerning a former soviet agent, code name Maid Marian, who originally came from behind the iron curtain over the Berlin wall.

(He has his notebook out and makes reference to it on the words curtain and wall.)

FAYE: *(Laboriously punching three keys)* C ... I ... A.

SOUTH: I suspect the aforementioned Maid Marian has seduced – *(Giggles etc. from BR1)* correction – is seducing Ambassador Douglas. Request a British secret service agent contact me. Recognition codeword, let's see now, let's use number – er – nineteen, "Turn on the spotlight." Have you got that Miss Baker? Turn on the spotlight. *(Voices off – at the front door)* Later, Miss Baker, I need to secrete myself in an advantageous listening post.

(Exit French window.)

(Enter front door, PERKINS, JOE, now wearing new trousers, and DEBBIE.)

PERKINS: I did also say I would not lie to the ambassador. You do remember that don't you Miss Deborah?

(FAYE gets up, knocks papers on the floor. PERKINS picks them up, takes FAYE's hands in his and gently sits her down so as to avoid the next disaster.)

DEBBIE: That's fair enough Perkins, but what's the harm?

(DEBBIE and JOE to the sofa. DEBBIE L. and JOE R.)

PERKINS: Oh, none at all I suppose Miss Deborah, but why did you have to say he was my brother?

(SOUTH is just visible listening outside the French window.)

DEBBIE: It was the first thing that came to my head.

FAYE: *(Now staring at her keyboard)* How do you spell virgin?

JOE: What a strange question.

FAYE: He told me to contact a long-legged virgin.

(SOUTH reacts.)

PERKINS: I don't imagine there's very many of those around these days.

JOE: Especially with the ambassador running loose.

FAYE: What does seduce mean?

PERKINS: Ahem! Faye my dear, we still haven't made those sandwiches. Why don't you come and help me. *(Turning to JOE)* As for you young man, if everyone is depending on my absolute discretion not to reveal your true identity, *(SOUTH reacts)* may I ask that you too be discreet, and stay out of the ambassador's way.

JOE: You can count on that. *(Exit PERKINS and FAYE to the kitchen)* Now Debbie, there's something I need to tell you about your father.

DEBBIE: *(Gets up, stares at the kitchen door, and takes three or four steps towards it)* "FAYE MY DEAR." Did you hear that?

JOE: What?

DEBBIE: Perkins with Miss Baker.

JOE: Never mind Perkins and Miss Baker, I need to talk to you about your father.

(Gets up and moves above the sofa.)

DEBBIE: Do you think it possible there could be something going on?

JOE: That's what I'm trying to tell you, something is definitely going on.

DEBBIE: *(Finally turns away from the kitchen door)* What makes you so sure?

JOE: Well, in the first place he can hardly keep his hands to himself.

DEBBIE: You know you're right. I noticed that myself earlier.

JOE: And in the second place, he keeps putting a move on me.

DEBBIE: No!

JOE: Oh yes.

DEBBIE: Perkins? I can't believe it.

JOE: No, your father.

DEBBIE: Perkins keeps putting a move on my father?

JOE: No, your father –

DEBBIE: What about him?

JOE: I don't think he's quite the person you think he is.

(SOUTH reacts.)

DEBBIE: I do hope you're not going to say anything nasty about Daddy.

JOE: Nasty? Me? About Daddy? *(Sighs)* Oh, what's the use – no my love, I'm not going to say anything nasty about Daddy. Forget it, let's get our things and get out of here.

(They get up.)

SOUTH: *(Stepping into the room)* I'm afraid nobody leaves here until certain investigations are completed.

JOE: Now look here –

SOUTH: Sit down if you please sir. *(DEBBIE sits R. end of couch. JOE perches on the R. arm)* I think we need everyone in here to answer a few questions. *(He strides to the kitchen and opens the door)* Miss Baker, could you step in here please? And you too Mr. Perkins. *(They follow him back into the L.R. FAYE sits at her desk and takes out a nail file. PERKINS goes to the chair indicated by SOUTH)* Now, where's the ambassador? *(A loud shriek and giggle from MARIAN in the bedroom)* Oh yes.

(He knocks on the door of BR1.)

HARRY: *(Off)* Who is it?

SOUTH: It's me, Captain South.

HARRY: *(Off)* What do you want?

SOUTH: You're needed for an urgent security conference sir.

HARRY: *(Off)* Oh, very well – just a minute.

SOUTH: Would you please take notes of the proceedings Miss Baker.

(FAYE continues to file her nails.)

(Enter MARIAN and HARRY from BR1. He is straightening his clothing, she is tidying her hair.)

HARRY: Is this really necessary?

SOUTH: I'm afraid so sir.

HARRY: *(Sits center of couch. MARIAN sits to his L.)* Well hurry up. Let's get it over with.

SOUTH: *(While everyone else is now seated, he moves*

continuously around the room) Now, as you all know, there has been a bomb threat at the embassy. What we don't know is whether this threat is directed against the – er – establishment, as it were, or against the ambassador personally. However, I have some ideas on that subject myself. I have been savagely attacked twice in the past hour and have reason to believe the bomber is masquerading as someone else, and that someone is here in this room.

HARRY: That's impossible.

(Murmurs of dissent.)

SOUTH: And furthermore, I have substantial evidence indicating overtones of international espionage.

PERKINS: I say, are you sure?

(Murmurs of dissent.)

SOUTH: I am presently awaiting word from the headquarters of the Central Intelligence Agency and I have also requested the help of the British Secret Service. *(He looks at FAYE but she is busy filing her nails)* Now, if you don't mind we had better see some identification. *(Turns sharply to JOE)* Perhaps we should start with you sir.

JOE: *(Stands)* Me?

SOUTH: Yes sir. Do you have some identification please?

JOE: *(Fumbling in his pockets)* I don't believe I do, you see these aren't my trousers – wait a minute – what's this? *(He pulls out a small folder)* It's a driver's license. *(Reads)* Percival Porter Perkins. *(PERKINS winces)* Here.

(He hands it to SOUTH.)

HARRY: Captain South?

SOUTH: One moment sir. *(Examining the driver's license and moving L. above the sofa)* It would help if they put photographs on these things. Hmm. It says here sir that you're fifty-two years old!

(Comes D. between MARIAN and PERKINS.)

JOE: Ah. Yes. Well. Remarkably well preserved, don't you think?

SOUTH: Yes sir. I do. *(He moves D.S. a little and faces R. to JOE. PERKINS in the chair is now directly behind him)* Would you mind telling me your birthday sir?

JOE: Well it's a bit personal really, *(PERKINS is holding up one finger of one hand and four of the other. Visible to JOE but not to HARRY and MARIAN, who continue to look R. towards JOE)* – er – er – it's the fifth. *(PERKINS shakes his head and holds up one, then four)* It's the fourteenth.

(Pause)

SOUTH: Yes?

(PERKINS nods.)

JOE: Yes.

SOUTH: The fourteenth of what sir?

(PERKINS is holding up nine fingers. JOE counts.)

JOE: September.

SOUTH: Hm. That's right. *(Hands him back the license)* I thought you said your name was Marc Anthony.

DEBBIE: *(To the rescue, as JOE looks blank, getting up and moving R to him)* Well, it isn't really, but we all call him Marc Anthony. I mean if you had a name like Percival Porter Perkins wouldn't you rather be called something else?

(PERKINS glares at her.)

SOUTH: Possibly, but – Marc Anthony?

DEBBIE: He's fond of making speeches.

SOUTH: So – I have revealed your true identity, Percival Porter Perkins.

PERKINS: Do you have to keep saying that?

SOUTH: Well everything seems to be in order.

HARRY: Captain South?

SOUTH: Yes sir.

HARRY: We're not all here.

SOUTH: We're not?

HARRY: Josephine. She's missing.

SOUTH: Good heavens you're right, and what's more, I think she was there when I was attacked.

DEBBIE: I think I saw her in the garden. If you're finished with Marc Anthony here, why doesn't he go and look for her.

(She signals behind her back, to JOE to go out and come in.)

JOE: Right, I'll find her. I won't be a minute.

(Exit, French windows.)

SOUTH: *(Follows JOE almost to the French windows)* I'm going to keep an eye on that young man. *(He returns DS.R. side of sofa and stands behind the sofa facing DS. left. During the next several lines, JOE reappears in the French windows, and firstly tip-toeing behind SOUTH's back, and then on all fours, makes his way to BR2)* Now, I'm not sure you all realize how serious this situation is. I want you all to understand that I am a highly trained security expert. Nothing escapes my attention. My eyes are everywhere, my ears are like finely tuned radar antennae. *(He turns L. towards PERKINS)* So, if anyone has any ideas about putting one over on me I advise them to forget it. *(He abruptly turns R. a second too late to see JOE go into BR2, as DEBBIE strikes a nonchalant pose in the doorway. Turns to HARRY)* And now sir, I would like to question your maid.

HARRY: Marian?

SOUTH: Yes indeed sir.

HARRY: I can assure you that won't be necessary. I can vouch for her personally.

SOUTH: Nevertheless, I have reason to believe she's not who she says she is.

HARRY: That's ridiculous. I absolutely forbid you to take this any further. Marian is my maid and that's the end of it.

DEBBIE: I think I hear Josephine in the bedroom. *(She opens the door to BR2)* Are you there Josephine?

JOE: *(Off)* I haven't finished putting on my eye shadow.

DEBBIE: If you put on any more eye shadow, raccoons will mate with you.

(JOE appears in the doorway of BR2. He is wearing the wig and fastening a large bath robe which reaches almost to

the floor. He has rolled up his trouser legs one turn, and is barefoot.)

JOE: Now what?

DEBBIE: Leave it to me. *(To SOUTH)* I can vouch for Josephine, she's a personal friend of mine.

SOUTH: I really need to see some identification Miss Deborah.

DEBBIE: Don't be stupid. Do you think this sweet, charming, innocent girl, *(JOE smiles sweetly and innocently, and curtsies)* could possibly be a mad bomber?

SOUTH: Very well, but I shall want to talk to you all again later. For the moment, I think I need a few minutes with you sir, in private.

HARRY: Very well, let's go in the study. Marian my dear, why don't you help Perkins in the kitchen.

(Exit HARRY and SOUTH to the study. PERKINS and MARIAN to the kitchen.)

DEBBIE: Come on. We'd better get you properly dressed.

JOE: I'm not putting that dress on again.

(They both exit BR2 and close the door.)

FAYE: *(Now alone on stage, starts to tidy her desk. It is somewhat cluttered with the computer keyboard, console, two telephones, file folders, etc. She picks up the console and places it on the floor in front of the DS.R. corner of the desk. The red phone rings. FAYE picks up the other one.)* Hello.

(The phone rings again) Hello. *(The phone continues to ring. SOUTH enters from the study, trips over the console and sprawls unconscious on the floor)* Hello. *(The phone continues to ring, FAYE looks puzzled then a sudden realization hits her as she figures out what is wrong, and she moves the phone to her other ear)* Hello. *(The phone continues to ring. She finally does figure it out and picks up the right phone)* Hello. Who? Oh, Captain South. *(Looks at him)* I'm afraid he's out. Oh, he's supposed to be here? Well he is here – I can't – because he's out – *(Pause)* I'm Miss Baker. *(Holds the phone away from her ear)* There's no need to yell at me. *(Listens again)* They hung up. *(She replaces the console on the desk and opens the kitchen door)* I'm afraid he's done it again, could you lend me a hand?

(Enter PERKINS and MARIAN.)

PERKINS: Really Faye, my dear. How did you manage it this time?

FAYE: I didn't do anything, honestly.

MARIAN: He's really going to believe there's a mad bomber now.

FAYE: Well we can't just leave him lying here. Maybe we should put him on a bed somewhere.

PERKINS: You're probably right. Let's get him into the bedroom. *(They manage to pick him up. FAYE and PERKINS at the head R., MARIAN with his feet L. They grunt, groan and struggle)* Here we go.

MARIAN: He weighs a ton.

FAYE: I know now why my mother told me never to pick up a marine.

(They exit to BR1 and close the door.)
(Enter cautiously from BR2, JOE still in wig and bath robe, as HARRY opens the study door and sees him.)

HARRY: *(Advancing with outstretched arms)* Josephine!
JOE: Oh no!

(He runs out of the French windows, pursued by HARRY.)
(Enter from BR1, PERKINS, MARIAN and FAYE. They all cross to the kitchen.)

PERKINS: Why don't you help us with the sandwiches Faye. That way we can keep an eye on you.
FAYE: Good. I always like to help.
PERKINS: *(Stops dead in his tracks, turns with his hands up. This in turn stops FAYE and MARIAN. Pause)* Well, maybe if you just watch!

(PERKINS, FAYE and MARIAN exit kitchen.)
(Enter running through the front door, JOE. He looks behind him, hurriedly closes the door, crosses to the L. side of the couch, whips off the robe and wig, sits on them and crosses his legs nonchalantly as HARRY bursts through the front door.)

HARRY: Ah, Marc Anthony. Have you seen Josephine?
JOE: Josephine? Oh yes. She just went thataway.

(He points to the French windows.)

HARRY: Thanks. *(He runs out the French windows)* It's definitely tonight Josephine.

JOE: *(Gets up, gathers up the wig and robe and knocks on the door of BR2)* Debbie.

DEBBIE: *Comes out of BR2)* Oh, there you are. Where did you get to?

JOE: There's something I must tell you about your father.

(Enter SOUTH from BR1 holding his head and limping. He staggers forward and leans on the back of the couch. JOE moves smoothly from DEBBIE's L. to her R., and opens the door of BR2 into which he steps just a fraction so as to be hidden from CAPTAIN SOUTH.)

SOUTH: I've been attacked again miss.

DEBBIE: Oh, dear. Do you have any idea who it is?

SOUTH: I'm pretty sure it's that Marc Anthony fellow. When I catch him I'm going to tear him limb from limb. *(JOE starts to put on the wig and robe)* You haven't seen him have you?

DEBBIE: Er – not recently.

SOUTH: Well, when I catch up with him we're going to see a little of the third degree. I'll beat the truth out of him. He doesn't realize who he's up against. Doesn't he know we're trained to kill in twenty-seven different ways?

JOE: *(Shudders and emerges from behind DEBBIE)* Ah, there you are captain. How are you making out in your search for the mad bomber?

SOUTH: Have you seen that Marc Anthony character miss?

JOE: Yes. I saw him sneaking out of the French windows a few minutes ago.

SOUTH: Right. I'll have to outflank him.

(Exits running, French windows.)

JOE: Now listen Debbie, about your father –

DEBBIE: What about him?

JOE: He's after me.

DEBBIE: What ever do you mean?

JOE: He keeps trying to – er – you know –

DEBBIE: No, I don't know.

JOE: Well, let's put it this way. I think he's a sex maniac.

DEBBIE: Daddy?

JOE: Well, every time he sees me he seems to get excited.

DEBBIE: Daddy?

JOE: Yes, for heavens sake, "Daddy".

DEBBIE: Excited?

JOE: Yes.

DEBBIE: His idea of excitement is waiting for his arteries to harden.

JOE: I can assure you –

DEBBIE: I don't want to hear any more. I'm not going to stand here and listen to you making disparaging remarks about my father. I'm surprised at you for even suggesting such a thing. I'm very disappointed in you.

JOE: Oh no! Now YOU'RE mad at me, hormone Harry out there can't wait to get his hands on me, and Captain Kangaroo is planning to kill me twenty-seven different ways. *(Pause)* Why do I feel like the only tree in a kennel?

HARRY: *(Enters from the front door and sees JOSEPHINE)* Ah, my dear. *(JOE takes a step back)* Debbie, why don't you help the others in the kitchen?

JOE: *(Quickly)* I'll come with you.

HARRY: No, no, my dear. Debbie knows where we keep everything, don't you sweetheart?

DEBBIE: O.K. Dad.

(Exit kitchen.)

JOE: *(Backing off around the R. side of the couch as HARRY approaches)* Really Mr. Ambassador, don't you think you're a bit old for this sort of thing?

HARRY: Not at all. I feel like a twenty-year old. The trouble is I can never find one available.

JOE: What makes you think I'm available?

HARRY: *(Lustfully)* It's the way you walk.

JOE: The way I walk? You mean like this? *(JOE puts one hand on his hip and does a slow "sexy" walk. HARRY mimics him. They speed up)* Oh my – HELP. *(He runs out of the French windows followed by HARRY. Enter PERKINS from the kitchen with a tray of sandwiches. He crosses R. to the credenza. JOE is heard off-stage, yelling)* DEBBIE – DEBBIE.

(DEBBIE comes out of the kitchen and opens the front door. JOE rushes in pulling off the wig and robe which he shoves at DEBBIE who slips them behind her back. JOE sits nonchalantly on the chair. PERKINS remains stock still, holding the tray, as HARRY runs in through the front door. JOE, PERKINS and DEBBIE all point to the study. HARRY runs into the study as SOUTH appears in the open front door. He sees JOE.)

SOUTH: You!

(JOE runs out of the French windows with SOUTH in pursuit.)

DEBBIE: Perkins – Quick.

(PERKINS puts down the tray. DEBBIE hands him the robe and they stand either side of the open front door. JOE runs in. DEBBIE gets the wig on his head. PERKINS gets the robe on him and he sits nonchalantly on the couch.)

SOUTH: *(Enters the front door at the full run, then stops just inside the front door and a little to its L. He looks around, but Marc Anthony is not there)* Damn!

(FAYE opens the kitchen door which flattens SOUTH against the U.S. wall. The kitchen door swings slowly closed. SOUTH stands upright for a moment, rocks back then staggers forward and finally falls unconscious as the curtain falls.)

CURTAIN

Scene Two

(Later that same evening.)
(It is now dark outside. The French windows are closed. The coffee table has been removed. The pull-out couch is now a bed with only the sheets on it. As the curtain rises SOUTH, his face and hands now blacked with camouflage paint, creeps furtively in through the French windows. He closes the door behind him, as JOE, now

minus the wig and robe, opens the door of BR2. SOUTH ducks behind the sofa-bed. JOE crosses behind the bed as SOUTH, first pulls him down out of sight, then, with a blood-curdling yell, flings him over the back of it onto the bed. SOUTH follows JOE over and grabs him, holding one of JOE's arms behind his back.)

SOUTH: Got you! Now I shall get the truth out of you.

JOE: Alright, alright, I give up. What in heaven's name do you want?

SOUTH: *(Leaning over him)* Now I'm going to make you talk. Now I'm going to find out the real secret of your identity.

JOE: Never. I will not compromise the honor and reputation of the woman I love.

SOUTH: I'm a highly trained interrogator. I can make you talk!

JOE: Never. You can put me in a little square room. You can tie me down in the chair. You can turn on the spotlight –

SOUTH: *(Stops dead in his tracks)* What?

JOE: What, what?

SOUTH: What did you say?

JOE: I said you could put me in a little room.

SOUTH: No – no. After that.

JOE: I said you could tie me in a chair and turn on the spotlight.

SOUTH: Good heavens. You!

(Lets JOE go and stands L. of the bed.)

JOE: Me?

SOUTH: You're an agent.

JOE: Well – er – yes.

SOUTH: I must apologize. I had no idea.

JOE: Apologize? What for?

SOUTH: Well now that I know you're an agent, things are different.

JOE: They are?

SOUTH: Of course.

JOE: You mean you're not going to interrogate me?

SOUTH: *(Laughs and moves R. above the bed then D. the R. side)* Of course not. I know now, without reservation, that as trained professionals you and I can travel this difficult road together.

JOE: *(Now sitting at the foot of the bed)* Actually, I usually do recommend reservations.

SOUTH: Now we should definitely make plans to catch them red-handed.

JOE: Them?

SOUTH: The ambassador and the maid.

JOE: You mean – ?

SOUTH: *(Gravely)* Yes. They are definitely working undercover together.

JOE: Well, I did think they were a bit familiar with each other.

SOUTH: Tell me, what time did you get here?

(Sits to JOE's R. at the foot of the bed and takes out his notebook.)

JOE: Oh, about half-past six, I suppose.

SOUTH: So – you've been on to him all along.

JOE: Who?

SOUTH: The ambassador.

JOE: Oh yes, I'm definitely on to him.

SOUTH: What made you first suspect him?

JOE: I suppose it was when he said we could make the earth move.

SOUTH: Ahah! – The bomb.

(Leaps up and goes D.R. a little.)

JOE: What?

SOUTH: I'm beginning to understand.

JOE: I'm glad YOU are.

SOUTH: You realize of course she's in disguise.

JOE: Don't you think it's a bit obvious?

SOUTH: What?

JOE: For the maid to disguise herself as a maid?

SOUTH: No, you see, she's not really a maid. She came over the wall and now she's a maid in England.

JOE: Made in England?

SOUTH: Now, does the ambassador know who you really are?

JOE: No, but he's come close to finding out a couple of times.

SOUTH: Good. Now I think we should give him a free hand.

JOE: If you give him a free hand I know where he's going to put it.

SOUTH: *(Now pacing above the bed)* Now I think our strategy should be to play along with him.

JOE: *(Follows him U.S above the bed)* What do you mean "our strategy"? You can do whatever you want, but I can assure you I have no intention of playing anything with that dissolute diplomatic disaster out there.

SOUTH: Nevertheless, I think we should give him plenty of rope.

JOE: *(Getting excited)* Plenty of rope? Have you any idea what he's liable to do with plenty of rope?

SOUTH: Alright sir, but I think we should definitely let him feel his way around.

JOE: *(Incredulous, almost screaming)* Feel his way around?

SOUTH: Yes, and then we catch him with his fingers in the cookie jar and *(He smacks his right fist into his left hand)* we spring the trap.

(JOE doubles over almost feeling the pain.)

JOE: *(In desperation)* Couldn't we spring the trap before he feels his way around?

SOUTH: Absolutely not.

JOE: That's easy for you to say. It's not your cookie jar he's got his fingers in.

SOUTH: Right. Now that we're working together, I shall keep you informed of my every move.

JOE: That will be a great comfort to me, I'm sure.

SOUTH: Remember now.

(He smacks his right fist into his left hand again, JOE winces.)

(Exit SOUTH through the French windows. JOE shakes his head and exits BR2. Enter from the study, HARRY now wearing pajamas followed by FAYE and MARIAN.

MARIAN is wearing a silk robe obviously borrowed as it's much too large for her, and FAYE, looking very attractive, is in a lace nightie. They are carrying a bedspread and pillows. The girls proceed to make the bed as HARRY moves about the room.)

HARRY: I think we can all be very comfortable, considering the circumstances. Let's get everyone in here and we'll decide who's sleeping where. *(He opens the kitchen door)* Perkins, would you come in here please? *(He continues pacing US)* Yes. If we're properly organized, the evening may well turn out to be highly satisfactory. *(PERKINS enters and stands by the kitchen door. FAYE smiles at him)* I think we can work this out to everyone's satisfaction. *(He is now at the door of BR2. He opens it an inch or two)* Debbie, have you got a minute please? Now let's see, who's missing? Ah, yes. Now where the devil has Captain South got to?

PERKINS: I saw him a short while ago sir, cowering behind the rose bushes muttering something unintelligible about a flanking attack at dawn.

HARRY: I see. Would you see if you can find him please Perkins?

PERKINS: Certainly sir.

(Exit front door.)

(Enter DEBBIE from BR2. The bed making now completed, DEBBIE, FAYE and MARIAN all sit on the bed. DEBBIE R., MARIAN C. and FAYE L.)

HARRY: Now girls, let's see where everyone will be. Debbie, you'll be in your room of course and I'll be in mine. There's this bed here and the couch in the study.

DEBBIE: Why doesn't Josephine take the study?

HARRY: Well I was thinking she might be better in here. It's a little closer to where I am. I'm sure she's a little nervous and would prefer the comfort of having me close by.

JOE: *(Entering from BR2 now in wig and robe)* On the contrary, I should definitely prefer to be in the study.

(He sits in the chair.)
(Enter PERKINS through the front door. He stops and turns.)

PERKINS: Now where's he got to? *(Calls outside)* Captain South! *(SOUTH appears)* What were you doing?

SOUTH: I just paused for a moment.

PERKINS: Oh no! Not on the begonias again!

HARRY: Ah, there you are captain, we're just making all our sleeping arrangements. I'm afraid it's going to be rather crowded.

SOUTH: Don't make any arrangements for me sir. I shall be on watch all night.

HARRY: Oh dear. What will you be watching?

SOUTH: I shall be patrolling the perimeter sir.

HARRY: You mean outside?

SOUTH: Yes sir.

HARRY: That's good. That's very good. Now Perkins, where the devil is that brother of yours?

PERKINS: *(He looks, first at JOE, then DEBBIE, they don't know what to do, finally in desperation:)* If memory serves me correctly sir, doesn't your constitution contain an article called the fifth amendment?

HARRY: What's that got to do with anything?

PERKINS: Well sir, I would like to decline to answer on the grounds it might incriminate me.

HARRY: What on earth are you talking about?

PERKINS: I can see it now. I'm going to go to prison and end up married to whoever has the most cigarettes. Miss Deborah, would you lend me a hand with this conversation please?

DEBBIE: Daddy, why doesn't Perkins go and find his brother and have him spend the night in his apartment?

HARRY: Good idea.

PERKINS: Thank you Miss Deborah. *(Aside to JOE)* Stay away from hot pants Harry.

HARRY: What's that?

PERKINS: I said chances are I'll never marry. Goodnight miss, goodnight sir.

(Exit front door.)

HARRY: Excellent. Things are going to work out after all. Now where were we?

JOE: We had just decided I was going to be in the study – ALONE!

HARRY: Had we? Ah, well – I guess that's alright.

MARIAN: Well that looks like you and I here Faye.

FAYE: That's fine with me.

HARRY: Right – well – *(He fakes a yawn)* I think it's about time we all turned in. *(To SOUTH)* Don't you have to go and dig a foxhole or something?

SOUTH: That's a terrific idea sir.

(Exit front door.)

HARRY: Right then, I'm off to bed.

(He winks at JOE and exits BR1.)

DEBBIE: Goodnight Josephine. If you're lonely you know where I am.

(Exit BR2.)

JOE: Yes – Oh yes – right, goodnight.

(Exit study.)
(MARIAN gets into bed R. side still wearing the robe.)

FAYE: I'll get the light. *(She moves to a switch by the front door. All lights dim. She gets into bed L. side)* Goodnight.

MARIAN: Goodnight.

(There is a slight pause, then the door of BR1 slowly opens. HARRY appears and tip-toes to look over the top of the sofa-bed. He then crouches down and creeps to the study door. He stands, primps a little, smoothes back his hair and silently opens the door, enters and closes it behind him. Another pause followed by a tremendous scream from JOE.)

JOE: *(Off)* Mr. Ambassador!

(The following happens simultaneously: [1] JOE, in wig and robe, flings open the study door; [2] DEBBIE opens the door of BR2; [3] FAYE and MARIAN sit up in bed; [4] SOUTH bursts through the front door and switches on

the light. JOE then runs across R. to take shelter behind DEBBIE. HARRY then slowly and rather sheepishly appears in the study doorway.)

MARIAN: Harry!
FAYE: Mr. Douglas!
SOUTH: Sir!
DEBBIE: Daddy!
JOE: *(To DEBBIE)* Now do you believe me? *(To SOUTH as he crosses L. above the couch)* And where were you when I needed you?

(SOUTH mimes digging a foxhole.)

DEBBIE: What were you doing in the study?
MARIAN: Yes, Harry, what were you doing in the study?
HARRY: *(Thinking frantically)* Now, now, there's nothing to get excited about.
MARIAN: I'm inclined to agree with you, but I'm still willing to try.
HARRY: *(Recovering his composure)* I must have been – er – sleepwalking. Yes, that's it, sleepwalking.
JOE: You walked right into my bed.
HARRY: Well I – er – I was asleep.
DEBBIE: Oh come on, let's all get back to bed shall we?
JOE: *(To SOUTH aside)* The next time the trap is sprung I want you there.

(Exit HARRY to BR1, DEBBIE to BR2, SOUTH to the front door, JOE to the study.)

MARIAN: Come on, let's settle down.

FAYE: *(Gets out of bed and switches off the light by the front door, then gets back into bed L. side)* Goodnight.

(MARIAN just growls and turns over.)

(There is a long pause, then: [1] JOE opens the study door and creeps on all fours into BR2; [2] FAYE gets out of bed and exits silently through the French windows; [3] HARRY appears out of BR1, crouches down, and is headed for the study when he notices MARIAN is now alone. He stops, and is about to get into the bed, when he looks at the study and is torn with indecision. He finally tip-toes down to the study door, primps a little and exits to the study; [4] MARIAN gets out of bed and tip-toes to BR1; [5] The front door opens and SOUTH enters. He tip-toes down stage, side steps the kitchen door, so as to avoid getting within six feet of it, silently opens the study door and goes in closing it behind him. Another pause, followed by a loud yell from SOUTH.)

SOUTH: *(Off)* HELP.

(The following happens almost simultaneously: [1] MARIAN comes out of BR1, jumps over the back of the sofa and into bed; [2] DEBBIE pushes JOE out of BR2, he is putting the wig on as he leaps across the bed and into the chair. DEBBIE stays in the entrance to BR2; [3] SOUTH runs to the front door and switches on the light. They all stand still as HARRY slowly appears in the doorway of the study. They all look at him.)

HARRY: I – er – *(Crossing his legs)* I had to go to the bathroom, must have lost my way in the dark.

DEBBIE: Daddy.

HARRY: Yes dear?

DEBBIE: Go to bed.

HARRY: Good idea. *(Crossing UR toward BR1)* Where's Miss Baker?

MARIAN: I'm sure I don't know but I seem to have this bed all to myself now.

HARRY: Good. Good – Oh I see. That's good!

(He makes a sign to MARIAN.)

(DEBBIE and JOE make signs to each other. Exit HARRY to BR1, SOUTH to front door, JOE to study, DEBBIE to BR2. MARIAN goes to the light switch by the front door. All lights dim, she opens the door to BR1, beckons to HARRY, and blowing him kisses, backs off towards the bed L. side. HARRY appears, blows her a kiss, She moves down the L. side of the bed. HARRY tries to grab her. She holds her hands out in front of her as if to fend him off. He stops. She indicates he should go down the R. side of the bed. He does. She stands on the bed and seductively opens the robe facing R. to HARRY. He lunges forward. She fends him off. He stops. She takes off the robe and throws it US. of the bed. She is wearing a camisole and tap pants. He lunges forward. She fends him off. She disappears under the covers, wriggles, sits up holding up the covers, twirls the camisole around and throws it US. of the bed. He lunges for her. She fends him off. She disappears under the covers, wriggles, sits up, twirls the pants around and throws them US. of the bed. She then

indicates he may get into bed. There is much giggling and wriggling under the covers, then the phone rings.)

SOUTH: *(Bursting through the front door, picks up the phone)* Security. Captain South here. *(HARRY and MARIAN remain motionless totally under the sheets)* Yes sir. This line is secure. Yes. Yes. Very good. Five minutes. I'll have the ambassador standing by. Thank you. *(He hangs up the phone, switches on the light, closes the front door, and heads toward BR1. As he passes the bed he stops, pauses, and comes D. to the L. side. He pats a lump under the sheets)* Er – excuse me.

(MARIAN sits up clutching the sheet, bare shoulders visible.)

MARIAN: Do you mind!

SOUTH: I beg your pardon miss, but is the ambassador there?

MARIAN: Just a minute. *(She disappears under the covers. After a brief moment she reappears)* Yes.

SOUTH: May I speak to him please?

MARIAN: Just a minute *(She ducks under the sheet and reappears momentarily)* Can I give him a message?

SOUTH: I really need to talk to him personally.

MARIAN: Just a minute.

(She disappears under the sheet and stays there.)

HARRY: *(His head appears)* Yes. What is it now?

SOUTH: I must have a word with you sir.

HARRY: O.K.

SOUTH: In private, sir.

HARRY: Oh, I see. *(He pats the bump)* Marian, my dear. *(She appears still clutching the sheet)* Captain South wants to see me in private. Would you mind? *(MARIAN whispers in his ear)* Ah yes. Quite right. One moment please Captain. *(They both disappear under the sheet. There is a frantic movement for the longest time. HARRY now appears wearing only the pajama top which is just long enough to conceal what needs to be concealed. However, he clearly dare not bend even a little and moves in little shuffle steps while pulling down on the pajama jacket with both hands. Finally MARIAN emerges from the R. side of the bed. She is wearing HARRY's pajama trousers with the cord tied above her chest.) (To MARIAN)* Why don't you wait in there my dear. *(He opens the door to BR1. Exit MARIAN. To SOUTH)* Confound it man. What do you want?

SOUTH: Sir. I'm convinced the maid is not who she says she is.

HARRY: Don't start all that again.

SOUTH: You don't seem to realize how serious this could be. It's my firm belief that she's trying to seduce you.

HARRY: You're right! And if you'll stop playing at the Sands of Iwo Jima for fifteen minutes she's damn well going to succeed. Now, will you please get out of here and let nature take its course.

SOUTH: I'm afraid there's a call from Washington coming through any minute sir.

HARRY: Damn. What time is it in Washington?

SOUTH: Almost exactly eighteen hundred hours sir.

HARRY: What's that in real time?

SOUTH: Just about the cocktail hour sir.

HARRY: Good heavens. It must be important. *(The*

phone rings. HARRY shuffles L., picks up the phone) Ambassador Douglas here. Yes. I see. Very good. Thank you. *(Hangs up)* They've cleared the embassy. We can cancel plan "M".

SOUTH: Right, I'll go and get the squad organized outside. We should be out of here in five minutes sir.

HARRY: Good. Very good. You're going back to the embassy?

SOUTH: Yes sir.

HARRY: Now?

SOUTH: Yes sir.

HARRY: Good. You're finally going to leave me alone?

SOUTH: Alone sir?

HARRY: Goodnight Captain.

SOUTH: Goodnight sir.

(Exit French windows.)

HARRY: Why should I tell her plan "M" is canceled?

(He switches off the lights and shuffles to BR1.)

(JOE comes out of the study on all fours, still wearing the robe and wig. He is half way across to BR2 when the front door opens and LOIS enters. She is dressed, carrying her suitcase, as before. She switches on the lights. JOE freezes.)

LOIS: *(Gasps)* Oh, you startled me.

JOE: *(Stands up and looks around)* Hello.

(There is a long awkward pause. LOIS looks at JOE. He stands fidgeting with his hands.)

LOIS: *(Puts down her suitcase)* Perhaps you should explain.

JOE: Why does everybody keep asking ME to explain?

LOIS: *(Closes the front door and comes D.S. a little)* Well, when you come home to find a strange woman crawling across your living room floor, it's something you – er – tend not to ignore. If you see what I mean.

JOE: Home? You live here? *(LOIS nods)* Then you must be Mrs. Douglas?

LOIS: Yes.

JOE: *(Rushes over to her)* Oh you don't know how pleased I am to see you. Now that you're here he won't get these urges and there'll be no need to spring the trap.

LOIS: I'm sure that's wonderful. *(Pause)* Do you think you ought to tell me who you are?

JOE: You're Debbie's mother – right?

LOIS: Of course.

JOE: Then, I'm Josephine.

LOIS: Then Josephine, perhaps you would care to tell me why you're wearing one of my wigs?

JOE: One of YOUR wigs.

LOIS: Of course, I'd recognize it anywhere.

JOE: Well – er – Debbie and I were trying them on. We were doing – you know – girl things.

LOIS: I see. May I have it please.

JOE: Have it?

LOIS: Yes please, the wig.

JOE: You want me to take it off?

LOIS: That's the idea.

JOE: I'm not sure *(Shouting)* DEBBIE would want me to.

LOIS: Here let me help you find out. *(She crosses to BR2 and flings open the door)* Deborah, would you come in here please?

DEBBIE: *(Enters)* Mom. What a surprise. Oh. I see you've already met Jo – sephine.

JOE: She wants me to take the wig off.

DEBBIE: Whatever for?

LOIS: I'm not a fool you know, Debbie.

DEBBIE: Alright, I don't care anymore. *(Crosses L. to JOE)* Here. *(She whips the wig off JOE)* Now are you satisfied?

(JOE sits on the bed. R. side.)

LOIS: Just as I suspected. Now, Debbie, who is this young man?

DEBBIE: Really Mom. We thought you were away for the weekend.

LOIS: Obviously. Debbie, I'm shocked. I can't imagine what your father is going to say.

DEBBIE: Not much, I don't think.

LOIS: Well! I don't think I appreciate your attitude. Your father and I have done our best to instill in you some sense of decorum and morality, and the moment you think you have the house to yourself, you invite a man here. And, I don't even want to think about what he was doing dressed as a girl.

DEBBIE: Oh, Mom. Don't be so dramatic.

JOE: No, she's right, it would be better if I left. I'll get my things.

(He goes into BR2.)

LOIS: *(Crosses L. and sits at the foot of the bed)* Your father is going to be heartbroken. I don't know how I'm going to break it to him, after the fine example he has set all his life.

DEBBIE:*(Sits to her R.)* Oh, Mom. Don't be so old fashioned, it's the 1990's you know.

LOIS: I don't care what it is. I won't have you entertaining a young man in your bedroom in my house.

DEBBIE: Alright then Mom, I'll go with Joe.

LOIS: Under the circumstances I think it might be a good idea for you to leave, until I've had a chance to have a word with your father.

DEBBIE: Oh I'm sure you're going to have more than a word with him. *(Enter JOE from BR2, now minus the robe and carrying his bag)* You ready Joe?

(She gets up.)

JOE: Sure, come on Deb. We could try to explain but no one would believe what's going on in this house anyway.

(Exit front door just as FAYE and PERKINS are entering. FAYE is still in her nightie but PERKINS is totally transformed. He is wearing black silk pajamas, a scarlet smoking jacket and yellow ascot.)

LOIS: Perkins? Is that you? Miss Baker, good evening, what on earth are you doing here?

FAYE: *(Giggles)* We came to get something to eat.

LOIS: I'm sure that's fine, but why are you here?

FAYE: I'm here with Percival.

LOIS: Percival?

PERKINS: Yes, madam. I'm afraid that's me.

LOIS: You mean you and Miss Baker are – er –

PERKINS: Yes indeed madam.

LOIS: I had no idea.

PERKINS: It is rather sudden actually madam, it happened earlier this evening. You see we became – er – quite attached to each other.

(He pats FAYE's derriere.)

LOIS: Well I must say this place is full of surprises.

PERKINS: I dare say there's one or two more still to come.

FAYE: Percival says we're going to make beautiful music together.

PERKINS: *(Embarrassed)* Faye, my dear.

LOIS: That's alright Perkins, though I do suggest that you go and conduct your symphony some place else.

PERKINS: Of course madam. *(He takes FAYE's hand)* Come my little magnolia blossom.

(FAYE giggles. They turn US. arm in arm. Pause. PERKINS takes FAYE's left hand from around his waist, and places it firmly on his derriere. They exit front door.)

(LOIS picks up her suitcase and enters BR1. There is a slight pause.)

HARRY: *(Off. Screams)* AEIOOOW! LOIS!

LOIS: *(Storms back into the living room, still holding the suitcase which she drops UL. of the sofa)* Get out here you miserable philandering two timing lump of lechery.

HARRY: *(Off)* Now dear. Don't get upset.

LOIS: "Now dear, don't get upset." I'll give you upset. Get out here and bring that – that – that bare naked, brainless, besotted bimbo with you.

HARRY: *(Off)* I won't be a minute dear.

LOIS: That's right. You'll be ten seconds.

HARRY: *(Enters, still in his pajama top only. He takes mincing little steps while continuously tugging down the jacket)* Now dear. There's an explanation.

LOIS: "Now dear. There's an explanation." You're damn right there's an explanation, and I know what it is. You've got your brains caught in your zipper again. You – you – animal.

MARIAN: *(Enters. Now wrapped in a sheet)* Harry – Who is it this time?

LOIS: This time? – You mean there's been other times? Harry Douglas. I've had just about enough of you. Get out of this house and into the gutter where you belong.

HARRY: But, my dear –

LOIS: Don't "but, my dear" me. Remove your insignificant, low life, scheming, lower than a snake's belly, person from my sight.

MARIAN: Oh, you're good. You know you're wasted doing this, you should be negotiating for the P.L.O.

LOIS: *(Screaming)* OUT. OUT. OUT.

(She almost pushes them out the French windows.)

MARIAN: My, my. I do believe we're not welcome. Come on Harry, let's go to my place.

(Exit HARRY and MARIAN through the French windows.)

LOIS: *(She quickly closes the French windows and hurries to the front door, opens it wide, switches the lights on and off three times, then crosses above the bed and stands on the R. side of it looking at the front door. After a brief pause SOUTH bounds into the room)* Fluffykins!

SOUTH: Sugarpie! Did you get rid of everyone?

LOIS: Yes. Yes.

SOUTH: Our weekend together at last.

(Takes one step forward and throws off his cap.)

LOIS: My lover boy.

(Throws one shoe over her shoulder.)

SOUTH: Honeylamb.

(Takes one step forward and tears off his jacket.)

LOIS: My gentleman gyrene.

(Throws off the other shoe.)

SOUTH: It's R & R time baby.

(Hopping on one foot and tugging at a boot.)

LOIS: Now – my little leatherneck – now!

(Gets her suit jacket off.)

SOUTH: Yes! Yes!

(Takes another step forward, trips over LOIS' suitcase and falls unconscious to the floor as ...)

THE CURTAIN FALLS

FURNITURE & PROPERTY LIST

ACT I:

On Stage:

Small table with mirror above.

Couch (which must pull out into a sofa bed) and loose cushions.

Low backed easy chair.

Coffee table.

Desk. (on it:) Vase of flowers, white telephone.
(under it:) Identical vase, broken in two pieces and flowers.

Coat stand. (on it:) Lois suit jacket, Lois purse and raincoat.

Credenza. (on it:) Bottles, glasses, etc.; bar paraphernalia and silver tray.

ACT II:

Scene One: The action in continuous.

Scene Two: (strike:) Coffee table, plate of sandwiches. all of Faye's papers on the floor and tidy her desk.
(set:) Sofa bed with sheets.

ACT I:

Off Stage:

Jug of lemonade. (Perkins)

Small suitcase. (Debbie)

Small suitcase. (Perkins)

Tray. (Perkins)

Small package. (Marian)

Bottle of Dom Perignon unopened. (Perkins)

Bottle of Dom Perignon opened in an ice bucket. (Perkins)
4 champagne glasses. (Harry)
Overnight bag. (Joe)
Jar of caviar and crackers on a plate. (Harry)
Jar of caviar. (Harry)
Pillow. (Debbie)
Red telephone, computer keyboard, file folders, papers, steno pad. computer console, pens, pencils. (Faye)
Faye's second skirt. (Debbie)
Large scissors. (Debbie)

ACT II:
Scene One: Tray of sandwiches. (Perkins)

ACT II:
Scene Two: Bedspread and pillows. (Faye & Marian)
Sheet. (Marian)

PERSONAL

ACT I:
Lois: Gardening gloves, Garden shears.
Faye: Purse: (in it:) Tube of super glue, pencil, handkerchief, nail file.
South: Walkie-talkie.

ACT II:
South: Pad and pencil.
Joe: Driver's license.

COSTUME PLOT

PERKINS:

Gray pinstripe trousers
Dark vest
Long sleeve white shirt – French cuffs
Cuff links
Belt
Black shoes
Black socks
Short, bartender type apron
2 ties (one whole, one cut off)
Scarlet smoking jacket
Black silk pajamas
Gold or yellow ascot
Slippers

DEBBIE:

Floral print summer dress or blouse and skirt combo
Casual shoes
Windbreaker

LOIS:

Skirt and jacket suit
Blouse
Casual shoes

JOE:

Dark business suit
Dress shirt
Tie

Dress shoes
Socks
2 pairs of identical tan slacks (one with the front cut out)
Sport shirt
Casual shoes
Woman's dress
Woman's shoes – medium heels
Wig
Bathrobe
Dark trousers
Boxer shorts

SOUTH:
U.S.M.C. Captain's uniform (Tan)
U.S.M.C. Combat fatigues including boots, hat and belt
White t-shirt
White boxer shorts with a U.S. Flag on the seat

FAYE:
White ruffled blouse
2 skirts
High heel pumps
Black lace slip
Silk pajamas or nightgown
Slippers

HARRY:
Casual trousers
Long-sleeved shirt
Tie
Socks

Casual shoes
Undershirt
White boxer shorts with red hearts
Leopard skin Tarzan outfit
Raincoat
Pajamas

MARIAN:
Cocktail dress
High heel shoes
Complete French maid's outfit
Silk robe (oversize)
Lingerie (2 piece)

AUTHOR'S NOTE:

Depending on the relative sizes of Harry and Marian, it may be necessary to have a second pair of pajama bottoms, tailor-made to fit Marian, pre-set in the bed.